SILVER BELLS

MARGARET A. WESTLIE

ISBN 978-1-926494-29-6

Cover Design by A. Michael Shumate

CHAPTER ONE

Liz MacLean tucked her slim right foot under her slender left knee as she sat on the parlour floor. "I wonder why Grand left this place to us?" She reached for another book of wallpaper samples. "I would've thought the logical person to leave it to would be Allan, after all he is his son."

"Yeah, but Allan hasn't been around for years. I didn't even remember what he looked like, I hadn't seen him in so long." Cassie sat cross-legged on the other side of the area rug.

Liz laughed. "I know, I had to be introduced to him myself at Grand's funeral."

"Hard to say why we inherited. Grand was a funny one. I didn't think he took much notice of either of us." She flipped another page in her sample book. "Oh, look, wouldn't that go just lovely in here." She pointed to a garish swirl of red and purple roses climbing up a grey trellis and giggled.

"Now, Sis, be serious. We've got to decide today. That one at the wallpaper place warned me severely to have this stuff back by five today, and she's a cross one. She's liable to have the Mounties after us if I don't get it back."

"Okay, okay. Here's a reasonable one. How about that for this room and the one with the primroses and lace that you found, for the dining room?"

"Annie would have loved doing this," said Liz. "She always had such a good eye for colour and texture. Much better than either of us."

"She did, didn't she?" Cassie turned down the corner of the page of another pattern. "This one's a possibility too. What made you think of her now?"

"I don't know, I've been thinking about her a lot lately. Maybe it's just because Grand died and it reminded me of her funeral. It was the first one I was ever at, you know."

"Did it make as big an impression on you as it did on me?" asked Cassie. "All those people!"

"Yes, and most of them are dead now, too. A lot happens in fifteen years, doesn't it?" Liz scrambled to her feet and stretched. "Mm, I'm geting stiff sitting on the floor. How about a cuppa tea?"

"Did Grand leave us that too?"

"He left us everything, even his long johns," replied Liz. "We're mistresses of all we survey!" She skipped a few steps across the room.

"Well, all I can say is, I'm glad that he left us some money too," grumbled Cassie, rolling to her knees from her seat on the floor. "A school teacher and a secretary could never afford to do the renovations we're planning without help from somewhere."

A few minutes later the girls climbed the stairs with sample books and mugs of tea in hand. "I dread the thought of rooting out all those old closets," said Liz. "Dear knows what's made nests in there by this time. I don't think they've been cleaned out since Aunt Lizzie did it last."

"Grand sure missed her when she died. He was never the same again."

"He wasn't, was he," said Liz. "I remember Aunt Lizzie well. This place always smelled so good when she was here, all warm and spicy. Annie loved to stay out here."

She dropped her armload of books on the bed. "Now what shall we do to this room?"

"I think this was Annie's room when she stayed here." Cassie collapsed on the bed beside the books. "What d'you think she would have liked?"

"Yellow daisies and butterflies, I think." Liz surveyed the room then sat down next to Cassie. "D'you remember how taken she was with butterflies?"

"She was like a butterfly herself," said Cassie. "She was always flitting here and there, and always so gentle and happy."

"It's strange to think of her as our older sister, she never seemed to be the older one."

"I know what you mean, and now since she's been gone for so long, it's like she's still a child, and we've grown up." Cassie flipped through the sample book in silence for a minute. "Here's one that'll fit Annie's personality." She passed the book to Liz.

"Mm," said Liz, "I don't know. The background's a little dark." She turned the book this way and that to see what the light would do to the design. "I can't seem to get a good light on this here." She jumped up and held it up by the mirror on the dresser. "How does this look?"

"Much better. I think it'll do nicely."

Liz looked into the glass. "This mirror's in pretty good shape for being so old."

"It's the best one in the house." Cassie leafed through more samples. "Now for the hallway. I think this grey and silver stripe will look nice, don't you? Liz? Liz?"

Liz was standing in silence before the mirror gazing into it with rapt attention. Her features seemed to shift and change before her very eyes. I'm imagining it, she thought, on the edge of a nervous giggle. A shiver of apprehension rippled over her skin. Her features returned to themselves as Cassie's urgent call penetrated her awareness. She gave herself a mental shake and turned to Cassie. "What's that you were saying?"

"I was talking about wallpaper." Cassie stared at her sister. "What's the matter with you?"

"Nothing."

"You look awful strange for just nothing."

"I guess I'm thinking about Annie too much today. I thought I saw her in the glass." She shook her head at the memory. "Silly isn't it?"

"Yeah, silly," said Cassie. "You keep that up and people'll be saying you're as crazy as cousin Gertrude and her mother."

"Well, I'm not!" Liz frowned in the direction of the mirror. A flash of pink and a suggestion of a figure disappeared the instant she looked at it. She turned her gazed away quickly and grabbed a sample book. "Let's get on with this wallpaper business and get out of here."

A week later Liz and Cassie arrived at the house armed with buckets and mops and other cleaning equipment. A cold grey rain swept in off the Northumberland Strait. The yard was greasy with mud, and the last leaves of autumn dipped and swirled in the wind until they fetched up against the white picket fence that separated the barnyard from the front lawn.

"Phew!" said Liz shaking the water from her raincoat on the front porch. "What a nasty day."

"Typical November weather," said Cassie. She opened the door with the key she had acquired at the reading of the will. "Let's get inside and get a fire going."

"I hope there's wood," said Liz. "I didn't notice the last time we were here."

"There's wood. I remember seeing it. I'll go pump some water."

Presently the fire was going and the kettle was heating. Cassie hauled several more buckets of water to partially fill the hot water tank on the end of the stove. The girls took off their coats and hung them behind the stove to dry.

"It doesn't take long to warm up in here once the fire's going," said Cassie.

"It's a good stove and a good flue," said Liz. "It's a shame he didn't have electricity."

"He never wanted it. He said they were perfectly comfortable without it."

"That's not the reason," said Liz. "They were so far from the road that when the electricity came through here, the company wouldn't run it without having him pay for half of it. He got mad at them and wouldn't do it at all then. So they never did have a line run."

"How d'you know that?"

"I remember Dad talking about it when I was little. For some reason the story stayed in my mind. I was always a little afraid of Grand."

Cassie picked up a bucket and a couple of rags. "I'm going to start in here." She headed for the pantry. "I'll wash dishes if you'll wash cupboards."

"You're on. I hate washing dishes." Liz dragged a chair into the pantry and climbed up on it. "Boy, it hasn't been cleaned in here in ages," she said as a cloud of dust descended on their heads from the top shelf. "Oh, look, here's that little pitcher that Annie liked so well. I thought it was gone long ago." She lifted it carefully out of the corner and handed it down to Cassie. A moment later, "See what else I've found, Aunt Lizzie's sterling silver salt and pepper shakers. I haven't seen these since she was alive." She passed them down. "I remember she always used to use them on holidays when we'd all come out here for dinner."

"You remember so much more than I do." Cassie's tone was wistful. "I hardly remember what she looked like, and Grand changed so much after she died that I didn't like to come here anymore."

Liz handed down a pile of plates. "I remember what she looked like. She was plump and jolly and always glad to see us. The cookie jar was always filled. Grand liked his cookies."

"I seem to remember an apron."

"She always wore one," said Liz. "I think the only time she took it off was to go to church or to The River. They did all their shopping in Murray River."

"What relation was she to us?"

"She was Grand's wife, that's all. Grand was Dad's uncle, that's why we called him Grand, because he was our grand uncle."

"I didn't know that." Cassie rinsed dishes and piled them on the drain board. "I guess I just never thought about it. They were always just Grand and Aunt Lizzie to me."

"Did you know that Allan wasn't really their son?" Liz looked down from her task of cleaning the top shelf.

Cassie chuckled. "I guess I never questioned that either. But come to think of it, he doesn't look like us so I'm not surprised. Where'd he come from?"

"Aunt's family all came from New Brunswick. Her sister was going with a Frenchman from up Edmonston way and he got her in the family way and then abandoned her. Grand and Aunt Lizzie took her in when her father threw her out in disgrace. She had Allan here at the house, then she just up and left one day without the baby. So Grand and Aunt Lizzie brought him up. I guess he gets his darkness from his father." She shook her strawberry blond curls. "He sure didn't look like any of us."

"Nor act like us either, if I recall correctly," said Cassie.

Liz chuckled. "You're right! His darkness is more than just in his looks." A car door slammed in the yard.

Cassie peered out the pantry window into the grey rain-washed day.

"Allan?" said Liz.

"Right on," said Cassie. "I guess I'd better

let him in. I hooked the door behind me when I came in from the back porch."

"Well, Allan, is it wet enough for you?" Liz jumped down from the chair and offered him a damp handshake.

"Plenty wet." Allan's tone was gruff. "What're you two doing?"

"Cleaning cupboards," said Cassie. "I don't think they've been done since Aunt Lizzie was alive. What brings you out here?"

Allan shrugged one shoulder and shifted his dark gaze away from her. "I thought I'd have a last look around before I went back to New Brunswick. It'll probably be the last time I'm ever here."

"It needn't be," said Liz. "You're welcome to come and visit with us any time."

"Sure." Allan glanced at her from the corner of his eye. He then turned to stare at them in silence.

The two girls looked at each other. "If there's anything you want for a keepsake, Allan, you're welcome to it."

"Of course, anything at all," said Liz. "Just let us know so we won't be looking for it later."

Allan smiled a strange half smile. "No thanks, what I wanted isn't here any more." He turned on his heel and went upstairs where the girls could hear him walking from room to room. Presently they heard him come down again, the front door slammed, and seconds later they saw him pass the kitchen windows on the way to his truck.

"D'you suppose we should check upstairs in case he did something up there?"

"What would he do," asked Liz, "set the place on fire?"

"Dear knows, the mood he was in."

"I suppose it wouldn't hurt, although checking up on our own family seems a sleazy thing to do, don't you think?"

"Yeah, you're right," said Cassie, "but he's not really family, is he?"

Liz sighed. "Then let's get it over with, eh. There'll not be much light left for cleaning at the rate we're going." She headed up the stairs with Cassie close behind. A swift tour of all the rooms revealed nothing and the girls returned to their work.

"He's a strange one," said Cassie. "I wonder what he really wanted?"

Liz shrugged and began drying dishes. "I dunno. Probably nothing. He may just have wanted to see the place one last time like he said. After all, he was born and brought up here."

Chapter Two

So you're going to move out to your uncle's old place, are you?" asked Bob in the teacher's lounge one day.

"I guess so." Cassie rummaged in the bottom of the bag of cookies to find a whole one. "Yuck! Nothing but crumbs."

"Here, have one of these." Bob tossed her a brown paper bag. "Mom made them, and as usual, she packed more than I can eat." He leaned back in an armchair and propped his feet on the battered coffee table.

Cassie reached into the bag without looking, shrieked and dropped the bag on the floor where it split in two, dumping its contents at her feet. "It moved!" she gasped, her face white with fright. She stared down at the bag which continued to move rhythmically. Tentatively she stuck out a sturdily shod foot and touched it with her toe. It buzzed at her in response. She jumped back, then noticed that the cookies were only plastic discs. "You wretch! You think you're so funny." She flipped the bag over with the toe of her shoe to discover a bent bobby pin with a button on an elastic band slowly unwinding its last turn.

"Yup," said Bob, his expression smug. He took his last bite of cookie.

Cassie picked up the button device and the plastic 'cookies.' "When are you going to grow up?"

"Next year." Bob grinned a freckled grin at her.

"Next year might be too late," she snapped.

"Too late for what?" Angus closed the lounge door behind himself and joined Cassie on the sofa.

"For him to grow up," muttered Cassie. She threw the gadget down on the coffee table on top of the plastic 'cookies.'

"He got you too, did he?"

"Yes, he did." Cassie scowled in Bob's direction.

Angus spread out his sandwich on its wrapper of waxed paper then rose to pour himself a cup of coffee. "I hear you're moving out to the old place pretty soon."

"We're just cleaning now. We want to paint and paper before we move in."

"There's no electricity out there, is there?" asked Bob.

"No, that's another thing we want to do, even before we paper." Cassie went to boil the kettle to make herself a cup of tea. "Drat, the kettle is dry. Nothing's going right this morning."

"What's the matter? Did Uncle Angus take all the coffee?" teased Bob. "Here, let me make you some more."

"Not on your life," said Cassie. "I'll do without. Dear knows what you'd put in it. Besides, I wouldn't have time to drink it anyway."

"Here, I'll share mine with you," said Angus. He picked up a clean cup. "It's hot enough to kill any germs I might have."

"Thanks." Cassie smiled up at him. "I'm going to need that to make it through the afternoon. They're that wound up these days."

"I expect it's all the Hallowe'en candy," said Angus.

Cassie turned to Bob again. "Can I trust you to behave like a normal human being?"

"Of course!" A hurt look passed over Bob's face and was quickly gone. "I'd never do anything mean or destructive."

"What d'you call the button trick? You nearly gave me a heart attack. If you'd done that to Mrs. Docherty she'd have dropped dead in her tracks."

"I wouldn't have done it to her. She's practically an old lady."

"Not so old," said Cassie. "She has five years to go before retirement."

Bob's face reddened. "I'm sorry, Cassie. You're right. I shouldn't have done it to you either. Will you forgive me?" He dropped down to his knee in front of her and folded his hands in prayer position.

"Oh, Bob! Get up from there and act civilized!"

"But will you forgive me?" persisted Bob from his position on the floor.

"I'll forgive you, if you'll get up from there." Cassie covered the beginning of a smile with a frown.

"Let me walk you home from school?" asked Bob still on his knees.

Cassie sighed. "If you want to."

"Y'know, Bob, if you really like Cassie, you should cut out the practical jokes," said Angus after the bell had rung and Cassie had departed for her classroom.

Bob sighed. "I know I should, but women seem to reduce me to juvenile idiocy, especially Cassie. I'd like to take her out but I'm afraid to ask. I'm afraid she'll say no."

"If you keep behaving like an idiot, I wouldn't blame her." Angus refilled the coffee pot with water and plugged it in to heat. "I'd like to ask her out too, you know, and if you don't do it soon, I will."

Bob looked startled. "I thought you were going out with Kay Linkletter from Summerside."

"I am, but it doesn't hurt to play the field." He smiled secretively.

"Does Kay know?"

Angus shrugged. "It doesn't matter if she does or doesn't. We're not married and we have no understanding as such."

"I hope Kay understands that," said Bob seriously. "And I hope if you do ask Cassie out, that you make it plain to her too." He frowned. "I wouldn't want to see her hurt for no good reason."

"Boy, you've got it bad," teased Angus. "Don't be so serious, it's all in fun." He stood up to leave. "See you later, and remember what I said."

"Humph! Fun! Some fun for the one on the receiving end," muttered Bob.

§

Bob hung around the hallway outside Cassie's classroom door until all the children had filed out and gone down the stairs out of sight. It'd never do to get them talking. Nine-year-olds have such a perverted sense of humour, he thought. He took a deep breath and knocked on Cassie's door.

Cassie looked up from the homework she was correcting. "Oh, hi, Bob, I thought you'd be long gone by now. Your class leaves early, doesn't it?"

Bob blushed to the roots of his chestnut brown hair. "I was waiting for you." His voice hoarsened and he cleared his throat. "I was waiting for you," he repeated more normally. "You did say I could walk you home, didn't you?"

"Yes, I did say that," replied Cassie. "I hope I won't live to regret it."

"You won't." Bob sat down in the first chair

in front of Cassie's desk, his long skinny frame sticking out at odd angles from the small chair. "Whenever you're ready. I can wait if you're not finished."

Cassie began gathering up her books. "I can do this at home this evening. They don't need it back until day after tomorrow anyway." She began erasing the blackboard.

"Here, let me do that for you." Bob leaped to his feet bringing the desk up with him.

Cassie suppressed a chuckle when she saw the look of misery crossing his face.

He sat down again with a crash and managed to squirm his way out of the desk, his beige freckles engulfed in another hot blush.

Cassie handed him the extra eraser and together they finished dusting the blackboard. The silence was thick between them.

"I'll get my coat," said Cassie. She set down the brush. "I'll get one of the kids to clean these in the morning. It's their all-time favourite job."

Bob picked up her books and papers and

waited until she returned. Together they walked the few blocks to Cassie's apartment in the gathering dusk.

I feel like such a fool. I can't do anything right, thought Bob. I hope Angus drops dead. His thoughts churned in his mind as he thought about his self-perceived ineptitudes.

"D'you live far from here?" asked Cassie to break the silence.

"Across from the Experimental Farm. Dad used to work there before he died. Mom still lives in the old house. I kind of look after her. She's getting forgetful."

"How old a woman is she?"

"She'll be seventy-five her next birthday."

"Not so old. Is she safe to leave by herself all day like that?"

"Our neighbour looks in on her every few hours. She gets her lunch and makes sure she's dressed and clean. She's not so bad yet that she can't look after herself. She just needs to be reminded to take her pills and which meal comes next and to eat when it's time.

Little things like that. She still has her sense of humour. She forgets sometimes that Dad's gone so we have to remind her. I think she must dream about him at night and then he seems to be right here like always."

"She doesn't try to cook or anything, does she?"

"No, she was never big on cooking when she was in her right mind, so she doesn't seem too interested in it now."

"What did she do all her life?"

"She worked as a secretary until she retired. It was soon after that she started losing her memory."

Cassie stopped in front of an old two storey house. "This is where I live. I can see Mrs. Campbell peering out from behind the curtains so I won't linger long. Thanks for walking me home, Bob."

Bob cleared his throat, but before he could draw breath to ask Cassie for a date, the front door was shutting quietly behind her.

§

"I see Bob walked you home this evening." Mrs. Campbell cackled. She was always greedy for gossip. "A fine young man, a credit to his Ma and Pa. You won't go far wrong with a man like him."

"I suppose not," replied Cassie, "but he didn't ask me to marry him, you know. And anyway, we work together."

"You never told me that!"

There's a lot of things I don't tell you, thought Cassie. "I'll be moving out soon, Mrs. Campbell. Probably by the end of the month." Cassie squeezed past Mrs. Campbell's plump form and went to pick up her mail from the hall table.

"Moving out? Where're you going? Out to one of them fancy new places over by the mall, I suppose."

"No, actually Liz and I are fixing up my uncle's place out near Murray River. We hope to be in it by Christmas."

"You're a foolish girl. What'll you do about the roads in the winter time? How'll you get to school? Or home again for that matter if it starts to snow? What'll I do for a tenant?" Her plump body collapsed on the deacon's bench like a sack of flour.

"What'll you do for gossip, you mean?" Cassie stifled a wry grin. "I expect if it snows hard enough to block the roads out there, it'll block roads here as well, and vice versa, and we do have weather forecasts." Cassie's mild sarcasm went right past her landlady.

"Yes, but you can't believe them. If they say rain, it's sure to be sunny, and if they say sunny, it's sure to rain. I've seen it happen more than once."

"I'll bear that in mind." Cassie stifled a chuckle which ended in a sigh as she picked up her mail. It had been opened again.

§

"Y'know, my cousin's an electrician," said Bob one day as he escorted Cassie home from school.

"Oh?" said Cassie. Half of her attention was on the translucent pink sunset. "What's that got to do with anything?"

"You did say that you and Liz were going to wire the house out there, didn't you?"

"Yes, as a matter of fact, that's the next thing on the list."

"I think I can save you some money. I used to work with Jon in the summer to earn money when I was going to Prince of Wales. What I was thinking was that Angus and I could come out some weekend and put the wires in, and then Jon could come out and check all the connections and put in the fuse box. That way you'd only have to pay him for whatever time it took him to do that, instead of for the whole job."

"Is he allowed to do that?"

"As long as the job's been inspected by a certified electrician there shouldn't be any problem. Besides, he'll be glad of the extra money. His wife is having their third baby soon and Christmas is coming."

Cassie and Liz arrived at the old house early on Saturday morning. The sun sparkled off the water in the Northumberland Strait. Seagulls scolded and cried as they wheeled and floated in the stiff breeze off the water, their strong white bodies in sharp contrast with the blue of the sky.

"I'll give you a hand with the groceries in a sec," said Cassie. "I want to stop for a minute and enjoy the morning." She took a deep breath of the cold, faintly salty air. "Let's take a walk on the shore before we start."

"You go if you want to. I want to get started before the guys get here." Liz picked up a bag from the car and started toward the door with her key in her hand.

Cassie sighed. "Work first and then play," she muttered, She picked up another bag, slammed the trunk lid down and followed Liz into the house.

"I'm glad I made that pudding yesterday," said Liz. She settled her bag on the pantry counter. "I sure wasn't expecting to get the wiring done so soon. That Bob's a handy fellow."

"I hope so," replied Cassie. Her tone of voice held some doubt. "He can be a real klutz when he wants to be."

"But such a nice one," teased Liz. She hung her coat on the hook behind the stove.

"If you say so," said Cassie half under her breath. She was still thinking about the incident with the cookies. "I wouldn't take any closed bags from him though."

"Why not?" Liz had acute hearing.

Cassie's answer was lost as Bob and Angus arrived in the yard. The tires of Bob's small pick-up crunched in the frozen gravel. The truck bed was packed to overflowing with coils of wiring and tools.

Cassie shrugged into her coat again and

went out to greet them. "I hope you brought enough wire," she said.

"I hope so too," said Bob. "There's not as much there as it looks. The truck's too small. Jon thought I'd need two rolls of wire, so I may have to go back to town. I'll use this first though and we'll see." He began unloading the truck, "Grab that, would you please, Angus."

In an hour the work was well under way. "I'm sure glad this place has a decent cellar." Bob grunted as he pulled at a particularly stubborn wire. "In some of these old places there's only just a storage area and the rest is crawl space. I hate sliding around on my back in the dirt."

"Have you asked Cassie out yet?" asked Angus. His mind was far away from the job at hand.

"Huh?" Bob frowned. "No, she never gives me a chance. I've walked her home from school almost every day for the last few weeks, and she makes some excuse about her land-lady watching and hurries into the house."

"Who does she live with?"

"A Mrs. Campbell over on Gower Street."

"Old Sadie Campbell? I don't blame Cassie for running. Sadie's a menace when it comes to gossip and nosiness."

"Cassie says she opens her mail all the time. She says she's always spying on her." Bob gave another tug to the wire, then shoved it behind the fuse box to await Jon's expertise. "I'm sure glad we can help the girls with this project. I'll be a lot happier knowing that Cassie's out here instead of where she is now, even though it is a long trip every day."

"You really like Cassie, don't you?" said Angus.

"Better and better," said Bob. "She's a sweetie and a lot of fun too. I just wish she'd give me a chance to ask her out."

"Ask her sometime when she's least expecting it. That way she'll have to decide, and then you'll know for sure."

"Mm," said Bob. "I'm not sure I want to know for sure."

"Well, if you haven't asked her out by the time school starts again in the new year, I will." Angus picked up a screw driver and began flipping it in the air. "I mean that."

"I see," said Bob. "So I guess if I'm to have a chance with Cassie at all, I'd better get going, eh?"

"Yep, looks like it," said Angus.

At one o'clock Liz called everyone for dinner. "You guys can wash up in the porch. Take a dipper of water from the tank on the stove. It's cold out there but at least the water'll be warm." She went back into the pantry and returned with the roast on its platter. She set it on the table, moving the jam jar of daisies over to make room for it. The jar was warm to the touch. She stifled a shriek and jumped back.

"Cassie! Cassie! Get down here!" Liz was

almost beside herself with shock.

Cassie ran down the stairs two at a time at the sound of the fear in her sister's voice. "Whatever is wrong?" She skidded to a stop on the linoleum and followed Liz's pointing finger.

"Did you do that?" demanded Liz. Her face was sheep wool white.

Cassie put out a tentative hand and touched the white petals. "They're real!"

"Of course they're real," snapped Liz. "And I asked you a question."

"Now where would I get fresh daisies at this time of the year? Of course I didn't do it."

"Do what?" asked Angus coming in from the porch with his damp towel slung over his shoulder.

"What's all the commotion?" Bob had followed Angus at the sound of Liz's shriek.

Liz pointed silently at the jar of daisies.

"Very pretty," said Bob. "They sure make those silk flowers look real these days." He picked up the jar. "Why are they standing in water? Silk flowers don't need water. It's warm water too." He handed the jar to Angus.

Liz and Cassie exchanged glances. "They were real enough a minute ago," muttered Liz.

"Nonsense!" said Angus. He inspected the flowers more closely. "They're silk and always have been silk. Look, there's a tag on one of the stems." He pointed at the tiny writing. "It says made in Taiwan."

"They were real," said Cassie. "I touched them and they were definitely real." She nodded her head for emphasis.

"You girls have been working much too hard at this project. You're overtired. Sit down and have your dinner and we'll finish on the job, then this evening Angus and I will take you both out for supper and a movie."

Liz dropped into a chair, still pale and stunned by the appearance of the flowers. "Real or otherwise, where'd they come from?"

"Did you do this, Bob?" Cassie turned toward Bob with fury in her voice. "It'd be just like you to pull a practical joke on us and scare us out of our wits."

Bob looked hurt. "Of course, I didn't do this, whatever this is. I swore off practical jokes after you said what you did about Mrs. Docherty and her heart."

"What's the big deal, anyway?" Angus set the jar of flowers back on the table and pulled out a chair. "They're very pretty and make a right nice bouquet for the table."

"The big deal is, that if we didn't put them there, and you guys didn't put them there, where'd they come from? Poor Liz is as pale as a ghost and shivering. Do you want me to fetch your sweater?"

Liz shook her head. "I'll be alright in a minute. It's just the shock. I could have sworn they were real, never mind that they appeared from nowhere." She took a deep breath. "The doors were all locked. I was just out to the porch, and I had to open the door to get to the trash barrel, and I know I left it locked behind me. The front door is locked too, because I went out there and locked it on purpose. I was afraid we'd forget to do it this evening and it'd be open all week."

"Well, sit in to the table, said Cassie. "The food's getting cold. Stay there Liz and I'll serve." She headed into the pantry passing Bob on the way. "If you did this," she whispered fiercely, "I'll have your guts for garters!"

CHAPTER THREE

"They say wall-papering is a true test of the strength of a relationship," said Angus. "D'you think you and Cassie'll make it?"

"Time'll tell," Bob steered around a red pothole. "And who are they anyway?"

"Those who know, I guess. Did you ever ask her out?"

Bob smiled. His pale features warmed into a faint blush. "Last Saturday."

"Oh, ho! So where'd you go? I take it she agreed to go."

Bob's face lost some of its happiness. "I had to promise I wouldn't play any practical jokes."

"The lady knows you only too well."

"I haven't played any practical jokes for over two weeks. Not since the cookies. I don't know why it takes so long to establish a new reputation." His frown was fierce.

"Two weeks is not very long considering that you've been a practical joker since kindergarten."

Bob slowed for the turn into the lane. "No, I suppose not, and patience was never my strong suit either. I just hope she sees how hard I'm trying. The temptation is awful sometimes."

"So where'd you go?"

"I took her to that new seafood place for supper and then we went to the Confed Centre for a concert."

"I'm impressed! That must have set you back a bundle."

"It was worth it."

"So did she let you kiss her goodnight?"

"That's for me to know and you to find out." Bob's tone was short and dismissive. He pulled abruptly to a stop in the farmyard.

§

Cassie greeted them at the door. "Hi, guys. We're just getting ready to start. Liz's been hard at it already this morning clearing out the room. Hang your coats up and I'll be up in a minute as soon as I finish here." She avoided Bob's eyes.

"I can stay and help you," he said.

"It's just dishes." Cassie still did not look at him. "I'll be through in jig time." She picked up her dish towel and went back into the pantry.

"I'll stay and keep you company, then." Bob followed her into the tiny room.

"There's not much space in here." A faint pink stained her fair skin.

"That's alright," said Bob, "I don't take up much space horizontally, and I'm right handy at reaching high places."

Cassie giggled as she looked up at Bob's skinny six foot something height. "You'll have to work."

§

"Oh, my aching back." Angus set down his end of the dresser. "They sure made heavy furniture those days. I suppose the bedstead is just as solid."

"It's oak," said Liz, "but it comes apart."

"Thank goodness." Angus went back into the bedroom and surveyed the remaining furniture. "Were you and Cassie going to move this stuff by yourselves?"

"Sure. It's the only way it would have gotten moved." Liz began tugging at the mattress. "Give me a hand with this. It needs to go out next before we take the bed apart."

"Bob tells me that he took Cassie out to dinner the other evening."

"He did?" Liz dropped her end of the mattress in surprise. "That little scamp! She never told me a thing about it."

"Does she usually?"

"Well, you know, sister stuff." Liz picked

up the mattress again and dragged it a few more feet. Angus pushed from his end. "We're going to have lift this over the threshold."

"I'll do it." Angus hurried to Liz's end of the task and together they heaved it over the door sill.

Liz propped her end against the hall wall. "I've already got the closet cleared out, all we have to do is get the bed out here and strip the old wallpaper."

"That's the fun part. Where do we start?"

"It really doesn't matter, it all has to go." She ran her fingers down a seam. "Here's as good a place as any." She lifted a corner of the old paper and peeled.

"There must be at least five layers here," said Angus. He began peeling on the other wall.

"There would be," said Liz. "Aunt Lizzie said that wallpaper kept the wind out, so she never took any of it off. I'm sure some of this stuff belongs to the first owners. It must be at least one hundred years old."

"Well, would you look at that." Angus

stood back to more easily take in what the wallpaper had been hiding for so many years. "I wonder who that is?"

"What did you find?" Liz turned to see. She gasped. Her spatula clattered to the floor. She stood gaping at the life-like portrait of a young girl with red-gold curls. It was painted directly on the plaster.

"What's the matter? D'you know her?"

Liz didn't answer. The portrait seemed to be smiling at her.

"Liz! Liz! What's the matter?" Angus shook her firmly by her arm.

Liz continued to stare open-mouthed at the portrait.

"Come away from this now!" Angus' alarm sounded in his voice. He turned her gently by the elbows and led her out of the room, closing the door behind them.

Liz burst into tears.

Angus took her into his arms and patted her awkwardly on the back. "There, there, now. There, there, now." It was a litany left over from his childhood and all that he could think of to say.

After a few minutes Liz's tears eased and she began fishing in her jeans pocket for a tissue. "Sorry, Angus," she managed to gulp on the end of a sniffle. "I don't know what came over me."

"D'you know the person in the portrait?"

Liz sniffed again. "I can't possibly know her. The portrait's too old." She didn't meet Angus' eyes.

"But she looks like someone you know?" Angus tipped her face up to look at her directly.

Liz nodded. "She looks very like my sister, Annie."

"Which one's she? I've never met her, have I?"

"She was our older sister. She died quite a long time ago."

"Oh." It was all Angus could think of to say.

"She drowned in the brook down by the bridge. She was just seventeen. She was beautiful."

"I wonder what her portrait's doing on the wall?"

"It can't be her portrait, it's much too old. The wallpaper on the bottom layer has to be original, so it just can't be her portrait. It must be someone who looked like her. The Mac-Leans all have that funny shade of red-gold hair, and the generations look surprisingly alike, even from the very first photos."

Bob and Cassie came clattering up the stairs. "What's up, guys?" asked Cassie. "Why're you standing out in the hall in the dark?" She flipped on the hall light and dispelled some of the gloom created by the closed door.

"We found something interesting under the wallpaper," said Liz. "So come and have a look and see what you think."

Cassie opened the door to Annie's room then stood stalk still on the threshold. "Holy cow! It's Annie!" She went slowly over to inspect the picture more closely. "How'd she get there?" She reached out a tentative hand and touched the likeness. "The paint's still wet!"

"What?!" The others tumbled into the room behind Cassie. "It can't be!"

"Well, it is." Cassie touched it again to make sure. Her fingers came away as blue as the dress she had just touched.

"But I just pulled the paper off that spot not five minutes ago. I did it with my own two hands," said Angus.

"There must have been four layers of paper on there, too," said Liz. "I know because my strip stuck and I had to scrape it off."

"The wall must be damp," said Bob. "I remember my mother saying one time that if you paper too soon after the wall's been plastered, that it'll never dry tight. Somebody must have painted that picture there and then papered over it too soon."

"That must be it," said Liz. She heaved a sigh of relief for such an easy explanation. "I guess I just panicked, she looks so much like our Annie."

"Well, that mystery's solved," said Cassie. "Let's get on with the job. I love to peel wallpaper. It's such fun."

"D'you remember the time you peeled that big patch off by your bed when you were little?" asked Liz.

"Indeed I do. I remember what I got for doing it too. Mom was mad that time." Cassie picked up a spatula and stuck it under the edge of a strip of paper.

"That was just before she got so sick," said Liz.

"I know. I thought for a long time that I'd caused her to get sick because I'd been a bad girl."

"I never knew that. What made you pick at the paper anyway?"

"D'you remember she and Aunt Lizzie and Aunt Maggie were spring house cleaning? They'd done Aunt Maggie's house and they were working on ours. Then they were going to come out here and do Aunt Lizzie's house but Mom got sick? Well, they'd finished my room, but I don't think the paper was new. I thought I'd help them by pulling it off for them, because that's what they'd done in the parlour and the dining room and in your room. I honestly thought they were going to do the same in my room, and that I was just helping them."

Liz chuckled at the memory and then grew serious. "That's the only time that I remember Mom being angry with us. I think she probably wasn't feeling very well even then. She was always the soul of patience. You cried for hours after that spanking and so did Mom. I don't think she'd ever spanked any of us before."

"I got the last piece." Cassie tugged on the paper. It came down readily and landed in a heap at her feet.

"What're you going to do with it now?" asked Bob.

"Use it for setting the fire, I guess. It's certainly dry enough." Liz began rolling the strips into neat bundles. "Waste not, want not."

"I'll start painting the woodwork," said

Angus. "What colour are you going to use?"

"That white paint. We'll do the accents afterwards."

"This'll be ready to paper as soon as the paint's dry."

"I expect we'll be able to start on it tomorrow if that patch of plaster's dried out then." She turned to look at the portrait again and gasped. "It's gone!" She sat down in the middle of the floor and stared at the wall. "There's not a trace of it!"

Angus brushed the place where the portrait had been with the backs of his fingers. "It's dry. I expect it faded when it dried out." He looked more closely at the plaster. "You can't even see where it's been."

"Thank goodness for that," said Liz. "I'm not sure I could have slept in here knowing that Annie was under the wallpaper." She scrambled to her feet with an assist from Angus. "I'll take these rolls of old paper downstairs and then get the vegetables ready for dinner. If you guys want to, you can move some of the furniture out of Allan's old room so we can start in there this afternoon."

Chapter Four

I'm sure glad we put in electricity," said Liz. She was sitting on the floor energetically applying paint to a baseboard. "We wouldn't be this far ahead if we couldn't work in the evenings."

"Nor so exhausted in the daytime either," said Cassie. She painted dark green highlights on the closet door in Grand's room.

"C'mon now, you know you've enjoyed every minute of it, and we'll soon be able to move in here."

"I hope so. I'm heartily sick of my landlady. D'you know she opened all my mail again the other day?"

"No, you didn't tell me." Liz rubbed at a run

in her painting job with a paint-stained rag.
I wonder what she hopes to find out?"

"I dunno, I've got nothing to hide. Bob
walked me home from school again the other
evening, and she was peering out the window
at us the whole time. I don't know what she
thought she'd see."

"Maybe a little koochie koo?" asked Liz.
Her glance in Cassie's direction was coy
and teasing.

"With Bob? Not on your life! His lips are
so wet all the time it's a wonder they don't
freeze shut."

"I heard from a reliable source that you
and he were out to supper the other evening"
Laughter lurked in Liz's voice. "C'mon, tell
big sister the details."

Cassie glanced out the corner of her eye at
Liz. "There aren't any details to tell. He took
me out to supper and then to a concert at the
Confed Centre."

"Where'd he take you for supper?"

"Gretchen's."

"Wow! That place is pretty pricey. I'm impressed."

"So was I," said Cassie. "I felt a little guilty about spending his money but he seemed eager to do it."

"I think he's right interested in you."

Cassie blushed and sighed. "Yes, but am I interested in him?"

"And are you?" Liz balanced her paint brush on the edge of the paint can then stood up and stretched.

Cassie sighed again. "I don't know. If I thought I could trust him not to play practical jokes on all and sundry I might give it a whirl and see how we get along."

"But he hasn't played any since he's been coming out here," said Liz.

"He doesn't dare." Cassie's tone was fierce. "He knows he'd be out the door in two seconds flat if he tried anything. I can see him chafing at the bit though. He was just dying to make something of that portrait business the other day."

"But he didn't. Besides, what could he have done?"

"Oh, I don't know, he'd think of something." Cassie threw her paint brush forcefully into the empty paint can. "There, I'm done. How about a cuppa tea?"

"Good idea, I'm parched. Put the kettle on. I'll be done here in a minute."

A short time later the girls were seated in Grand and Aunt Lizzie's old rocking chairs with their stockinged feet propped up on the open oven door, mugs of tea in hand.

"Y'know, I've been thinking," said Liz.

"Have you, now," teased Cassie. "What's that like?"

"Something like sex?" Liz laughed. "Seriously, I have been thinking. We should have a family get-together over the Christmas holidays. You'll be off school until after New Year's, and my boss is taking his family to Florida for the holidays. We could invite all the cousins and Aunt Maggie and Uncle Will, and ..."

"And we're so far off the road, one good snowstorm and we'd be here for a week with all of them," interrupted Cassie.

Liz sighed. "I suppose you're right." She thought for a moment. "I know! We'll rent snowmobiles and taxi them in from the road. They can park their cars in the field there, and when the plow comes through they'll be able to leave."

"Good idea, but can you picture Aunt Maggie on a snowmobile?" Cassie's eyes sparkled with mischief at the thought.

"Or Uncle Will either." Liz chuckled. "You'd have to wear a suit of armour with him on the back. He'd be trying to feel up the driver."

"They probably wouldn't come anyway."

"What about Allan? Should we invite him?"

"We'd better. He'd be insulted if he didn't at least get an invitation, and he's by himself. I don't think he has a girlfriend."

"I can't see him with a girl somehow. Can

you imagine making out with him?" Liz shuddered involuntarily. A sound of cracking china emanated from the pantry.

"What was that?" Cassie's feet hit the floor with a thud as she sat upright in her chair. The girls jumped to their feet and hurried into the pantry switching on the light as they went. Milk was spreading slowly across the counter from the china cow.

"Look at that!" Liz picked up the little pitcher. "There's a hole right through the side of it." She stuck her little finger through the hole. "It's like it had been punched out with something."

"That's the strangest thing I've ever seen!" Cassie peered inside the pitcher. "There's not even a chip of china inside. I wonder what made it do that?"

Liz mopped up the leaked milk. "I don't see a chip here either. We can't even glue it back together."

"Maybe it'll make a good planter. We can put some 'Old Man's Whiskers' in it and put it up in Annie's room."

"She'd like that, I think," said Cassie. The kettle sighed on the stove, just on the edge of boiling.

The girls resumed their seats in the kitchen. Outside, the wind from the Strait whistled and moaned around the eaves. "Sounds like it might snow tonight," said Cassie. "Wouldn't that be fun? Snowbound up here with no telephone, and no way out 'til the plow came by."

"Yes, and no blankets, and no breakfast, and no way to get to anything until the plow came by either," Liz pointed out.

"Maybe we should have a phone line run too," said Cassie. "If we ever got a very big storm we'd be really isolated. Are you sure you want to invite all the cousins?"

"Well, maybe not all the cousins."

"What about Gertrude and her husband?"

"I don't know about her. I've only seen her the once at Grand's funeral since we've grown up. She seems nice enough, and not a bit strange like her mother was. She has a little boy, you know."

"Maybe she wouldn't want to come. Remember how awful we were to her when we were kids?"

Cassie sighed at the memory.

"I remember locking her in the barn one day with the pigs. She was terrified of pigs."

"She wasn't until you and Allan got through telling her what mother pigs would do to her if she went near their little ones."

"That was an awful thing to do to a city girl, wasn't it?" Liz laughed. "It's a wonder we didn't warp her mind that time. She was just beside herself. I still feel a little guilty about that!"

The girls fell silent for a few minutes. Presently Liz said, "Did you ever notice that this family hasn't been the same since Annie died?"

"I don't really remember what it was like before she died. I was too young. I just remember Mom and Dad talking about how different it was before, but I thought they meant around our house."

"I remember. I also remember that Allan left right after Annie's funeral and hasn't come back 'til now either."

"So?"

"So, if you put that together with the fact that Uncle Will and Aunt Maggie and Murdoch were here that weekend too and haven't visited much since then either, I'd say something serious happened."

"Like what?"

"Like something to do with Allan's hasty departure. I wonder how much Maggie and Will had to do with it?"

"Liz, that's pure imagination! I'm surprised at you."

Liz shook her curly head. "No, it's not my imagination, and I don't know why I didn't think of it before. This family got along fine when I was little, and now they never have a thing to say to each other. In fact, those three would make a u-turn in the middle of Great George Street to avoid having to talk to each other. And it all started just about the time

Allan left here."

"I still think it's your imagination," said Cassie.

"Look, you just admitted that you were too young to remember what it was like before. I was eleven and I was very aware of what was happening in the family. That was the year that Mom was so sick and I was doing the housework. They started thinking of me as an adult that year and weren't so careful about what they said around me. There was some big mystery about Allan and why he left."

Cassie looked intrigued. "What d'you think it was?"

"I haven't any idea. They never did come right out and say it in front of me, but whatever it was, it caused a rift in the family." Liz paused for breath. "It has never made much sense."

"D'you suppose it had anything to do with Annie?"

Liz made a face. "Allan was never really one of us somehow when we were young. I don't know what it was. Maybe he did something. Maybe they just thought he did."

"I can't imagine him drowning her." Cassie's horror showed in her expression and tone of voice. "Or Grand letting him get away with anything if he did do something to her."

"No, Grand was pretty fierce, alright," said Liz. "I guess we'll never know what really did happen, but I'd sure like to put this family back on track."

Cassie shrugged one shoulder. "Just invite them here for Christmas and see what happens. I don't think anything will, because I still think it's all your imagination."

"Oh dear," said Liz, "maybe we can't do all that over the holiday. I saw Gertrude downtown the other afternoon, and I asked her if they'd like to come and she said yes, if Don was free they would. I had the feeling that was an excuse. I don't think she likes the others either."

"She needn't know the others are here until she gets here. Besides, didn't her mother have the second sight? Maybe Gertrude can intuit the mystery for us if she's inherited the gift."

Moving day was cold and grey. Rain threatened all afternoon.

"I hope it holds off until we get this stuff moved in here," said Bob.

"I'm just glad I didn't have much furniture to move," said Cassie. "Books are bad enough."

"You and my back," said Angus. "If it's one job I hate, that's moving furniture!" He picked up a box and headed for the front door. Bob followed him with another.

"I think this is the last of the boxes," said Bob. He set his load down in the parlour with a thump. A flutter of white from out the corner of his eye caught his attention. A flower lay by the leg of Grand's armchair. It was a daisy. "This wasn't here before, was it?"

"I dunno," said Angus. "I didn't notice. It probably fell out of one of the boxes. The girls'll know where it came from."

§

Supper was a merry event that evening. Angus and Bob regaled the girls with every eerie story about old houses that they could think of. There was always a humorous twist to each one, although enough of the truth was told to send shivers down at least Cassie's spine. Bob sat in the rocking chair beside the stove and toyed with the silk flower he'd picked up in the parlour.

"What have you got there?" asked Cassie. "You've been playing with it ever since supper."

Bob waved it in the air. "It's only a silk daisy. I picked up on one of my many trips to and from the truck."

"Where'd you find it?"

"In the hallway, I think. Or was it in the parlour? I don't remember. It was kind of pretty and I picked it up so it wouldn't get dirty." He stood up and stretched. "I'm going to the john and then I think we'd better hit the road for town, Angus. It's starting to rain out there, and it could freeze."

"Have you thought any more about a Christmas get-together here?" asked Cassie after the guys had left.

"A little." Liz gave the kitchen table one last wipe before rinsing the dish cloth and hanging it on the line behind the stove to dry. "I thought we'd better not invite any more than we have beds for, if it does storm that day."

"So if people don't mind doubling up, that would mean we could invite, um," she counted possible beds in her head, "about six or seven counting us."

"That's what I thought too, although I don't know who'd want to room with Will." Liz made a slight face. "I suppose we could put him on the lounge here in the kitchen."

"Good idea," said Cassie. She propped her stockinged feet on the oven door. "That way he'd be good and far from the rest of us."

"All the beds are three-quarter beds. I don't know how Maggie will cope, she must weigh about two hundred and fifty pounds."

"Two hundred and five," said Cassie. "She told me last week that she'd lost almost fifty pounds this summer."

"And I wanted to snowmobile her in here!" Liz sighed

"We could always put her on the sled and drag her behind," suggested Cassie. She was hard put to keep a straight face.

"You know, we should get a dog," said Liz.

"Good idea, then we could dog-sled her in." Cassie could no longer contain her chuckle.

"No, I mean wouldn't it be nice to have a dog for company here?" Liz got up from her seat in the rocking chair. "You really don't like her, do you." She reached for the teapot. "More tea?"

"Half a cup." Cassie held out her mug. "No, she's not my favourite person. Never has been. She was always criticizing and commenting on what I was doing when I was little. She constantly compared me to cousin Mary who, of course, always came out better than I did. I didn't know the difference until I was grown and I happened to mention it to Mary. She told me she did the same thing to her about me. We've been best friends ever since."

"Back to the question of the dog. What d'you think?"

Cassie shrugged. "It may not be such a bad idea. We're pretty isolated here. What if something happened?"

"What could possibly happen around here?"

"Look what happened to Annie. We'll never know for sure how it happened." A log fell in the stove and a draft seemed to move through the house. Somewhere upstairs a door slammed.

"I thought this house was practically airtight," grumbled Liz. "We put enough insulation in it."

"I wonder if someone sneaked in just to scare us?" said Cassie. She shoved her feet into her slippers and rose from her seat.

"I wouldn't put it past that Bob. He's been quiet too long. I think we'd better go and look. A dog would be right welcome now."

The girls crept quietly up the stairs. Liz held the frying pan and Cassie carried a stick of wood from the woodbox. A thorough inspection of the upstairs did not reveal anything out of place.

"All that panic for nothing." Cassie giggled in relief. "Sorry I misjudged you, Bob."

"Not exactly for nothing," said Liz. "What's this on the floor?" She bent down and picked up a daisy from the landing. "Bob dropped his flower."

"Those guys are playing tricks on us." Cassie scowled.

"I don't think this is a joke," said Liz. "This daisy isn't silk. It's fresh!" She stood staring at the fresh daisy in her hand.

"Fresh?! Not again. Let me see it."

Liz passed the flower to Cassie who looked at it for long seconds. "I wonder where it came from and why here on the landing?"

§

They awoke the next morning to a sparkling bright day. The frost had made paisleys on the window panes during the night, and an inch of snow covered the ground. The ravens cawed in the spruce trees behind the house. The world seemed all red and white and blue.

"Good morning." Liz stirred up the coals in the firebox left from the night before. She added another stick to the fire and clanged the stove cover shut. "Did you sleep well?"

"Like the proverbial baby." Cassie yawned and stretched. "What's on our agenda for today?"

"Finish unpacking, I suppose. It should be warm in here in a few minutes." She rubbed her cold hands together. "This is a good morning for porridge."

"Let me make it. I've never made porridge before and I want to try."

"Have at it," said Liz. "If it turns out badly, you're eating it."

"I won't know 'til I try." Cassie rummaged in the cupboard for a pot. "I watched Mom often enough, I think I can." She filled the pot with cold water and added some oatmeal and a little salt, then a little more oatmeal for good luck, then set the pot on the stove to warm. "There, that should do it." She sat down at the table rubbing the sleep from her eyes.

It was a few moments before her brain processed what her still drowsy eyes were looking at. She leaped to her feet with a gasp and stood stalk still in the middle of the kitchen staring at the table. "Liz! Come here quick!" she shrieked.

Liz hurried from the pantry with a handful of dishes. She deposited them on the table with a crash. "Not again. Are they real?"

"I dunno," said Cassie, "and I'm not going to be the first one to touch them." She folded her arms in front of her.

"Oh, don't be silly," said Liz, "they're only flowers." She reached out toward them.

"Boo!" said Cassie loudly. Her sense of

mischief had taken over after the shock. Liz jumped back. "Only flowers, eh?"

Liz glared at her then reached once more toward the daisies. "They're real," she said quietly. "I guess we do need a dog."

"Well, I'm going to search the house, and check the doors and windows," said Cassie. "Where's my stick?"

"I burnt it," said Liz. "You'll have to find another one." She picked up the frying pan. "I'll go with you."

"You just don't want to stay here by yourself," said Cassie. She rummaged in the woodbox for another weapon.

"You betcha," said Liz. She checked the back door. It was still locked. The girls toured the house and found everything to be closed and locked as they had believed it to be. "I didn't even see any footprints in the snow outside," she said when they had returned to the kitchen.

"That's no indication," said Cassie. "Whoever brought them could have been in and out of here before the snow even started."

Liz sighed. A worry line wrinkled her brow. "I suppose you're right. I don't know what we can do, we've already put dead bolts on all the doors and new locks on the windows. I don't understand how anyone could just walk in here anyway. They'd almost have to be Houdini."

Cassie tossed her weapon back into the woodbox and lifted the lid of the porridge pot. "Oh, dear, I think I used too much oatmeal." She picked up the wooden spoon and tried to stir the glutinous mass that filled the pot to within an inch of the top. The spoon stood upright in the center of the pot and refused to stir. She tugged at it but it stuck firmly in the porridge. "It's like cement." She began to laugh. "What am I going to do? How am I going to get it out of there? What am I going to do with it when I do get it out of there?"

Liz's serious blue eyes sparkled with rare mischief. "You could always slice it and fry it."

Chapter Five

Although the weather continued cold and damp well into December, snow did not enter the forecast again. Cassie and Liz made their daily trip in to Charlottetown, Cassie to teach her classes at the elementary school and Liz to carry out her duties as executive secretary to the head of the Department of Agriculture.

"Maybe we'll be lucky and not have snow 'til after Christmas." Cassie helped herself to nuts and a glazed cherry from Liz's mixing bowl.

"Green Christmas, fat graveyard, and keep your fingers out of that or we won't be having any fruitcake for Christmas dinner.

Aunt Lizzie always had fruitcake and this is her recipe."

"My goodness, you're not in very good trim today," said Cassie. "Come to think of it, you've been kind of sharp these last few days."

Liz looked a little ashamed. "Sorry. I haven't been sleeping well lately. Ever since we found that bouquet of daisies, it's been on my mind that we may not be safe out here by ourselves."

"Is that why you prowl around in the middle of the night?"

Liz's eyes widened. "I don't prowl. I never even get out of bed. I thought it was you!"

Cassie shook her head, a look of concern on her face. "It's not me either. Maybe we really should get a dog."

"That's probably the best answer. We can stop at the animal shelter on our way home on Monday and do a good deed as well as a good turn for ourselves." Liz continued stirring in silence for a few minutes.

"How many people are going to be here?" Cassie crunched happily on a spare walnut, her worries about intruders forgotten now that the problem of their safety was to be resolved so neatly and humanely.

"Aunt Maggie's coming. I guess we'd better give her the room off the parlour for herself. Uncle Will said he wouldn't come if Aunt Maggie did, so I told him she wouldn't be here. Gertrude and her husband and son are coming. They can have your room and you can room with me in Annie's room."

"What are Uncle Will and Aunt Maggie feuding about now, and what's he going to say when he finds out Aunt Maggie's here?"

"It'll be too late by then. He'll just have to put up with it." Liz knocked the batter off her wooden spoon against the side of the mixing bowl. "I'm going to get this family back together again if it's the last thing I do!"

Cassie made a face. "That should make for an interesting visit. What about Allan?"

"Oh, yes, I nearly forgot about him. He said he'd come."

Cassie reached for another glazed cherry

and Liz slapped her hand away. "Leave those alone."

"Well, that's a big surprise. By the sound of him a few weeks ago, he wasn't going to set foot on the Island again. Where're you going to put him?"

"He can room with Uncle Will. There're twin beds in his old room, so he won't actually have to sleep with him." Liz dumped the fruit and nuts into the cake batter and began folding them in.

Cassie chuckled. "I sure hope it doesn't snow."

Liz rolled her eyes. "Me too."

"Are you going to get presents for everyone?"

"Heavens, yes," said Liz. "I don't have time or money but can you imagine Aunt Maggie if there was nothing under the tree for her?"

Cassie sighed, "I suppose I'd better too, eh?"

A faint scratching sounded at the door. "What's that?" Liz paused in her stirring. "I hope we don't have rats. That's all we need."

Cassie went to the door and opened it.

A very thin, half grown dog sat looking up at her with pleading in his eyes. His shaggy coat was matted and dirty. Burdocks clung to the fringe of hair along the edge of his belly. He beat a hesitant rhythm on the porch floor with half of a tail and whined ever so quietly deep in his throat.

"Well, Mr. Dog, where did you come from? You look like you've been on the road for awhile. Do come in." She moved aside and the dog crept into the warmth of the kitchen almost on his belly and settled himself by the stove.

"I think we've found our dog," she said.

Liz turned and looked at the dog. "Not much of an excuse for a dog," she commented. "D'you suppose he'll guard for us?"

Cassie shrugged. "I dunno, but he needs a home and we have one. Is there anything in the pantry I can feed him?"

"There's some cold potatoes left over from yesterday's supper. He might like that. They're in the fridge. You can warm them with a little of the gravy."

Cassie rummaged in the refrigerator and found the potatoes and gravy. She mashed them together and stood stirring them over the stove. "When's our first guest arriving, and who is it?"

"Aunt Maggie, and she's coming next Sunday. She's all agog to see what we've done here and she couldn't wait 'til Christmas Eve."

"Nosy old biddy! I suppose she'll have plenty to say for what we should have done, whatever that may be in her estimation."

"Now Cassie, a person'd think you didn't like Aunt Maggie the way you're talking about her. We needn't have invited her."

Cassie sighed. "I know, but what's Christmas without an Aunt Maggie? And besides, you want to solve the family problem, don't you? I just hope she helps a little. She really is the salt of the earth." Cassie made a face.

"Even if she doesn't, Uncle Will will keep her busy. He likes stout women and Aunt Maggie was always a favourite of his to annoy." Liz tipped the fruitcake batter into a greased tube pan and scraped the bowl. "Is that stuff hot enough for the dog yet?"

"Oh, I forgot about it. It's probably scalding by now." Cassie tried a little on the edge of her lip. "I guess I'd better cool it down with some milk. It'll take the mouth off him, it's that hot."

Snow was falling softly, dusting the ground with white, when Aunt Maggie drove her ancient over-sized car into the dooryard. "You should have had the lane scraped while you were at it. I almost lost a muffler on the bridge."

"We're glad you could come, Aunt Maggie," said Cassie sweetly, giving her a dutiful peck on her wrinkled cheek. "Give me your car keys and I'll take it back out to the road again so you won't be snowed in up here."

"The forecast doesn't call for that much snow, and besides, I've been snowed in here more than once," she wheezed.

"I'm sure you have, Aunt Maggie," said Liz, "but would you really want to be snowed in again? After all, we are a long way from town and what if the power goes out?"

"You laid on power, did you? It's a good thing. I always told Grand that he should have electricity, but he was so stubborn." She lumbered onto the porch. "Well, at least you got that fixed." She pointed to the new board in the porch floor. "I cracked that two years ago when I was up here visiting and Grand never got it fixed. I was over three hundred pounds then and the board was rotted. Grand said it wasn't, but I know it was."

"Come in out of the cold," said Liz. "I have a fire going in the kitchen and the kettle's on the boil. We'll have a nice cup of tea to warm us up when Cassie gets back."

"Don't mind if I do," puffed Aunt Maggie, out of breath from the effort of walking from the car. "My, you two sure have fixed up the kitchen pretty, and so nice and clean too. You girls are a credit to your Ma, God rest her soul." She sniffed at the memory of Liz's mother. "Is the rest of the house this nice?"

"We think so," said Liz. "Let me take your coat." She assisted Aunt Maggie out of her coat and hung it behind the stove with her own. "Have a seat by the fire and get warm." She pulled the rocking chair over toward the stove and helped Aunt Maggie into it. "Cassie'll be back in a few minutes and we'll have a little tea. I made some sugar cookies this morning."

"Are they as good as your aunt's?"

"I hope so," said Liz. "She made the best ones I ever tasted." She spooned tea into the pot and poured boiling water over it just as Cassie returned.

"Look who I found at the gate," she said as she closed the door behind herself and her companion.

"Allan! Welcome! We weren't expecting you 'til tomorrow. Come in and get warm. I'm just making some tea." She set the pot on the side of the stove to steep.

"The forecast wasn't good for tomorrow so I came today. I hope you don't mind."

"Heavens, no," said Liz and Cassie in the same breath. "We're just glad you could get here at all." A whine issued forth from behind the stove.

"What's that?" Aunt Maggie craned her neck and leaned toward the stove, almost upsetting the rocker. "It sounded like a dog!"

"It is," said Cassie. "Come out here, Mr. Dog, and meet the people."

Mr. Dog crawled out from behind the stove on his belly and lay against Cassie's feet and whined.

"At least you don't have to teach him to lay down." Allan put his hand out to stroke Mr. Dog's head. The dog growled and made to snap at Allan's hand

"He's a cross one." Allan jumped back.

"No, he's not," said Cassie, "he's just frightened."

"Humph," said Aunt Maggie, "some watch dog. He can't even stand up to growl."

"He looks like Annie's old dog," said Allan.

"He does, now that you mention it," said Liz.

"Well," sniffed Aunt Maggie, "that was the only dog that Grand ever let in the house. He always said that animals belonged in the barn, and I agree with him." She sniffed again.

A rap sounded on the porch door, and Cassie went to answer it. "Why Gertrude, we weren't expecting you 'til tomorrow either. C'mon in." She threw the door open wider. "Here, let me help you with that." She took Gertrude's suitcase from her hand. "And this must be your son?"

"Yes, this is Roderick. Say how do you do to Cousin Cassie, Roderick."

"How do you do?" Roderick stuck out a small mittened paw to his cousin.

"My goodness, the red hair of him," said Aunt Maggie from her rocking chair. "He looks just like your great grandfather, Gertrude."

"I wouldn't know," replied Gertrude. "I never saw great grandfather. How are you Aunt Maggie?" She bent to kiss the powdery, wrinkled cheek. "It's been a long time since I've seen you."

"Yes, well, you know where I live."

"And Allan! I didn't see you standing there. It's nice to see you again. Are you here for the holiday then?"

"Don't sound so enthusiastic." Allan came out from his retreat on the far side of the stove. "Did your husband come too?"

"Oh, I almost forgot. Uncle Will's stuck out at the end of the lane. He drove that great big car of his into the ditch. Don's out there helping him get it out."

"Was he hurt?" asked Liz. Alarm tinged her voice.

Gertrude laughed. "No, just mad. The air was pretty blue when we arrived."

"Trust Will to do something like that," said Aunt Maggie, "and in broad daylight too."

"I've got a hitch on the truck," said Allan. "I'd better go out and help them out." He shrugged into his coat.

"Tell Uncle Will to leave his car at the gate in

case it snows," called Cassie as Allan slammed the door behind himself.

"Have you got your Christmas tree yet?" asked Don after supper that evening.

"We got it yesterday. It's in the parlour," said Liz. "I think, since we're all here early, we can decorate it this evening." She finished wiping up the kitchen table.

"Allan and I'll put it up," said Don, "and we'll all have a hand in decorating it." He headed toward the parlour.

Cassie carried boxes of ornaments and tinsel down from the upstairs storeroom. "These were all Aunt Lizzie's. Heaven knows what's in here." She plopped herself down on the floor and began rummaging through the box. "Here, Roderick, you can help me."

Roderick sat down on the other side of the box from Cassie. "This is pretty." He carefully lifted out a silver bell. "Listen to how it rings."

The faint sound of silver bells tinkled softly in the old parlour.

Cassie looked startled. There was only one bell and it had no clapper. "I think I'll put some Christmas music on," she said. She jumped to her feet. "You put the bell in a safe place, Roderick. It was Annie's favourite and I'd hate if it got broken."

Gertrude shook her head slightly at Roderick. "But I didn't do it," he protested softly.

"We'll talk about it later," said Gertrude sternly. "In the meantime, no more bells."

The evening passed swiftly. Christmas carols and laughter rang out until nearly midnight while the cousins renewed their acquaintance as adults. The girls chattered and reminisced. Allan said little, even when Don resorted to all his skills as a psychologist to try to draw him into conversation. Uncle Will made courtly passes at Aunt Maggie which she parried with maidenly blushes left over from her youth.

"I wish Murdoch was still here," she said to Liz after one such advance.

"Did you see Aunt Maggie actually flirting with Uncle Will this evening?" Cassie and Liz made their nightly round of checking the doors and windows. "I thought I'd die!" She put her coat on to take Mr. Dog out for a last run before locking the door.

"It must have been the eggnog." Liz chuckled. "I slipped a little rum into it and I don't think she drinks."

"Oh, no!" said Cassie. "You didn't! She's a teetotaller. She gave me a lecture on the evils of drink once. We'll have to make sure she never finds out."

"I'll never tell." Liz yawned her way upstairs.

Sometime in the night the snowstorm came howling in from the sea. Cassie wakened briefly as a particularly heavy gust of wind shook the house, then dropped back into a dreamless sleep.

Liz incorporated the sound of the gale into her dream of coldness and dark nighttime images. Her mother, deceased now for several years, appeared from the darkness and began stroking her forehead with gentle hands. Her image ebbed and flowed in Liz's sleeping thoughts as she closed her dream-time eyes and gave herself over to the mothering. The touch changed. Just how, Liz could not tell. The image was no longer her mother but the stroking continued, long cold strokes on Liz's warm forehead. Her uneasiness mounted to a nameless fear and she sat bolt upright in bed, stifling a shriek as she came to herself. Cassie slept on beside her.

"It's just the eggnog," Liz reassured herself and lay back down on the pillow. She stared into the darkness for what seemed like hours, her eyelids straining open until the darkness outside the window became less intense, announcing the approach of the grey stormy dawn.

I might as well get up and start breakfast,

she thought as she rolled quietly out of bed, careful not to disturb Cassie. She washed and dressed hurriedly and made her way downstairs to the lingering warmth of the kitchen. Coals still glowed in the stove from last night's fire. She stirred them and added some kindling and another log. The fire was soon popping and snapping as the sap heated and began to burn. It was a happy sound. Mr. Dog crawled out from behind the stove and came over to Liz wagging his tail.

"So you're awake, are you?" Liz bent to scratch his ears. "I do believe you're putting on some weight already. You're not a bad looking fellow now that we've gotten you cleaned up. D'you want to go out?" Mr. Dog's tail wagged even faster. "You'd think you knew what I'm talking about." Liz straightened and turned toward the door. She stopped in mid-stride as her gaze took in the bouquet of fresh daisies on the kitchen table. It was all she could do not to run and hide.

"Did you put those there, Mr. Dog?" she

said out loud to reassure herself that she wasn't dreaming. "Of course not. Silly me. Dogs don't pick daisies. Especially not in the middle of December." She reached out a tentative hand and gently touched a petal. "They're real!" She ran her hand over the jam jar they had been placed in. "It's warm! Annie always put her flowers in warm water." The gentle tinkle of silver bells filled the air. Liz backed carefully away from the bouquet and the sound of the bells faded.

She opened the door to let Mr. Dog out. "Don't be long." She thought about the flowers for long minutes. Mr. Dog scratched at the storm door to be let back in. "I'm going to make myself a cup of tea and pretend this didn't happen," she said out loud. "The others will be up in a little while, then Cassie and I can go someplace and discuss this quietly. Maybe by that time the flowers will have disappeared."

She sat for nearly an hour curled up in the rocking chair with her cup of tea. She stared at the bouquet willing it with all her strength to go away. The bouquet remained in its jam jar in the exact centre of the kitchen table. At seven o'clock Aunt Maggie joined her.

"You're up early," she cackled. "Was it you that was making all the racket this morning early?"

"I've been up since a little before six," said Liz. "Can I get you a cup of tea? I'll make breakfast soon. I can hear the others stirring." She uncurled herself from the rocking chair and headed into the pantry. She picked up a cup and saucer and returned to the kitchen to pour tea for Aunt Maggie. "What racket was there last night?" she asked.

"It wasn't last night," said Aunt Maggie. "It was early this morning. I distinctly heard it. Footsteps first, then it was like silver wind chimes, only I don't know if there is such a thing."

Liz's hands trembled on the cup, clattering it in its saucer. "Not around this house there isn't." Her voice was tight. The tea slopped over the edge of the cup.

"Goodness child, you've spilled the tea," said Aunt Maggie. "And you're as white as a sheet. Sit down here this instant before you fall down."

Liz slid gratefully into the rocking chair that Aunt Maggie vacated for her. "I'm sorry Aunt Maggie, I didn't sleep very well last night, and I've been working hard getting this place ready before the snow came. I guess I'm just tired out."

"It looks to me like you've had more than one sleepless night," scolded Aunt Maggie. "What's worrying you?"

Liz considered the cost of prevaricating. "I've just been very busy at work," she replied. "Then we'd come home and work here too. That's all."

"Well, you've certainly done a creditable job. I admire your taste. Even the daisies look real. That's a real nice touch. Silk daisies. They really brighten up a place."

Liz rose from her chair and went to examine the daisies. She swallowed hard to prevent the escape of a gasp. They were, indeed, silk!

§

Footsteps clattered down the stairs. "I forgot my shaving cream," said a bristly Allan. "Is there any left in Grand's mug that I could use?"

"Help yourself," said Liz. "It's there on the shelf behind the stove." She waved a fork in the general direction of the shaving mug.

Allan reached for the mug. "Grrr!" said Mr. Dog. His hackles rose.

Allan jumped back. "That dog is too cross." He reached for the mug again.

"Ruff! Ruff!" Mr. Dog snapped at his ankles.

"You'd think he didn't want me to use my own father's shaving mug!"

"I'll get it for you," said Liz. She set her fork down in the spoon rest on the warming oven door. She reached for the shaving mug and went to hand it to Allan. Mr. Dog was silent. "There, maybe he really didn't want you to have it." Just then the shaving mug cracked into two pieces. One piece fell to the floor and broke into several more. Liz stifled a shriek and nearly threw the other half after it. She stood for a few seconds staring down at the broken shaving mug, one shaking hand covering her mouth.

Allan's scowl was fierce and dark. "Maybe someone really doesn't want me to have Grand's shaving mug. Maybe I'm not supposed to have anything of Grand's." He turned and stomped off upstairs.

"Sit down child," said Aunt Maggie. She vacated her seat in the rocking chair for the second time that morning. "It's only a broken mug. No need to get so upset." She put her plump arms around Liz and led her to the rocking chair. "I'll sweep that up in a minute." She took the fork from Liz and went to turn the bacon. "You know, you really should see a doctor for your nerves. I had to do that right after Murdoch died. I wasn't sleeping so I threw myself into house cleaning to keep my mind occupied and to tire me out, but it didn't work. I finally went to the doctor and he gave me some little yellow pills. They really did the trick. I slept like a baby after that. Of course, you can't take them things too long or after awhile you'll need them. I'm as right as rain these days but I always keep a few around the house just in case."

Aunt Maggie babbled on. Liz sat in silence in the rocking chair, not even rocking. If things keep on like this around here, I'm going to need more than little yellow pills, she thought. She rose from her seat and took a deep breath to steady herself, then went to fetch the broom and dustpan from the porch. She swept up the remains of the mug. "I don't know what's gotten into Mr. Dog these days, he's never cross with us."

"Maybe he just doesn't like Allan," said Aunt Maggie. "The bacon's done. D'you want me to start the eggs?"

"No, wait until everyone comes down or they'll be tough." Liz dumped the broken china into the waste basket and put the broom and dustpan away.

"'Morning everyone," said Cassie as she came through the door. "What was all the noise last night?"

Liz jumped. "What noise?"

"I don't know. Uncle Will's up there grumbling about not being able to sleep with all the racket going on. I didn't hear a thing."

"No," said Liz, "you didn't even move when I woke up with a bad dream." She went into the pantry to get the dishes. "Here, you can start setting the table." She handed the basket of silverware to Cassie.

"More daisies?" Cassie frowned. "Where'd they come from?"

"They're silk." Liz's tone was short. "I have to talk to you after breakfast." She stomped off into the pantry to get the napkins.

"I'm going out to shovel off the porch so we can at least get the door open once this stuff stops." Allan's tone was gruff. His face was red and nicked in a couple of places. "Because of that dog I had to shave dry this morning."

"Thanks Allan," said Liz. "I see you did get shaved."

He shrugged into his coat. "Are the shovels in the same place?"

"I think so," said Liz, "I haven't had a chance to houseclean the back porch yet."

Roderick lay on the floor near Mr. Dog and played with his truck. Truck noises came and went. Gertrude and Cassie washed dishes in the pantry. Aunt Maggie sat rocking in the chair, silent for once.

"R-r-r-r," sang Roderick to himself. "Look out Mr. Dog, or I'll have to arrest you." He ran his truck up to Mr Dog's toes and screeched to a halt. He reached out and patted Mr. Dog's head. "Annie told me to give you a pat for her," he said. He began to sing to himself again. "Annie, Annie, beautiful little Annie."

"What's that you're singing?" asked Liz, who had only heard the last of the song. She stood very still staring at Roderick as she waited for his answer.

"I was just singing about Annie," said Roderick. He continued to run his truck and hum to himself.

"How do you know about Annie?" The tension in her voice communicated itself to Roderick.

Roderick looked up and shrugged. "I don't know."

"Tell us about Annie, Roddy." Gertrude came in from the pantry and scooped her small son into her arms.

"She was in my dreams last night."

"What did she look like?"

"Pretty." Roderick's reply was too brief.

Gertrude sat down on the lounge and settled Roderick on her lap. "What colour was her hair?"

"Yellow, I think. Sort of red too. Like hers." He pointed at Liz.

"Was there anything special about her?" asked Liz. She could not contain her anxious question for another moment.

Roderick looked up at Liz. "She was picking

daisies and she had a whole big bunch of them."

"Did she say anything to you?" Cassie's ears had been straining from the pantry to catch every word while she finished tidying up.

"She told me to give Mr. Dog a pat for her, only she didn't say it in words."

Liz frowned. "How did she say it then?"

Roderick shrugged. "I don't know, in my mind, I guess." He squirmed on his mother's lap. "I want to play with my trucks now." Gertrude released him and he went back to his place on the floor. He began running his toys using the space between Mr Dog's paws as a parking lot.

"Quite the imagination," remarked Aunt Maggie from her rocking chair. "He takes after his great-great-grandfather in more ways than in appearance. He had a wonderful imagination. He could sit and spin stories for hours and none of it true."

Liz ignored Aunt Maggie's reminiscences. "I think I'll build a fire in the parlour stove."

"I'll help you." Cassie scrambled to her feet. The two sisters went through to the parlour and closed the door behind themselves.

"What do you make of that?" asked Cassie.

Liz shivered in the coolness of the room. "I don't know, but that was certainly Annie he was describing."

"You don't suppose he's queer in the head like his grandmother, do you? She was always seeing things the rest of us couldn't."

"I don't think Aunt Agnes was queer at all. I think she just wanted the rest of us to think she had the second sight."

Liz stirred up the ashes from last night's fire hoping to find a few live coals. There were none.

Cassie scrunched up some newspaper and handed it to Liz. "I don't remember Agnes very well. She moved to Texas to live with Aunt Dolly and she only came back to visit that once when I was eleven."

Liz arranged kindling on top of the newspaper, then her hands lay idle on the edge of the cold stove for a moment as she thought deeply about the events of the past day. "I dreamed about Mom last night," she said at last. "Only it wasn't Mom. I mean it changed from Mom into someone else and I woke up."

"Phew! That most have been scary! Why didn't you wake me?"

Liz smiled slightly and picked up a spruce log and placed it on top of the kindling. "You were sleeping soundly, and it really was only a dream."

"But you were scared," observed Cassie.

Liz sighed. "It was the feeling of the dream, not the content, that scared me. I couldn't go back to sleep, so when it started to get light out, I got dressed and came downstairs. There was another bouquet of fresh daisies on the table." She paused. "At least I thought they were fresh." She struck a match and lighted the newspaper.

"What do you mean you thought they were fresh?" Cassie frowned at Liz.

"I mean they were fresh when I came down-stairs, and when Aunt Maggie joined me an hour later, they were silk."

"Wow!" said Cassie, "That is strange! Are you sure?"

"No," replied Liz. "That's the trouble, I'm not absolutely certain."

"Well, real or silk," said Cassie, "where'd they come from?"

Liz slammed down the cover of the stove and opened a draft. "I don't know, but there's other weird things been happening while you were asleep." She told Cassie of the incident of the shaving mug.

Cassie merely shrugged. "Coincidence," she said. "You probably just let it slip."

"I don't think so. It just kind of split and fell apart, and Aunt Maggie was complaining about the noise in the night. Footsteps and bells, she said, or wind chimes."

"Oh," was all that Cassie could contribute this time.

§

The storm continued all day. The wind howled in the eaves shaking the house with its force. Frost crept up the window pane despite the storm windows, until there was only a small crescent left to look through. At about five o'clock the lights flickered, then flickered again and went out.

"I'm glad we have the wood stove," said Liz. "It'll be awhile before they get the electricity back on in this gale."

"The oil furnace can hardly keep up with the cold as it is," said Cassie. "Even with all the insulation we put in, it's still drafty in here the way the wind is blowing."

"Will we have water?" asked Allan from his seat on the lounge.

"Oh, yes," said Liz, "plenty of water. We never took out the old hand pump. We just set up the electric pump beside it. There was plenty of room for them both."

"Did we buy candles at The River the other day?" asked Cassie.

"Yes, and kerosene and new lamp mantles too," replied Liz. "If you pass me down the lamp, Allan, I can fill it and we can have some more light in here now."

Don wandered in from the parlour where he had been passing the afternoon engrossed in a book. "Well, it certainly got dark all of a sudden." He chuckled. "What do you think of it all, Roderick?"

"I think it's going to be a long evening," replied Roderick in very adult tones. "I think Mr. Dog is right. We're going to see the light very soon."

Liz felt a shiver go down her spine. "How old did you say Roderick is, Gertrude?"

Gertrude laughed. "He's five going on one hundred and five."

"As I said before," said Aunt Maggie from the rocking chair, "he's got the imagination of his great-great-grandfather. Talking to dogs, indeed!"

"He plays by himself a lot," said Gertrude, "so he makes up events to pass the time."

"Wasn't making it up," said Roderick in a sudden fit of stubbornness. "I did talk to Mr. Dog."

"Now Roderick, remember what we said about not talking about your pretends to anyone besides Daddy and me."

"But Mommy, it's not pretend," said Roderick. "I really did talk to Mr. Dog." Roddy was on the verge of tears.

"What'd he say about me?" asked Allan. "Something good, I hope."

"He doesn't like you. He said you're bad and that you shouldn't be here." Roddy's tone was bold.

"Roderick Harvey!" said Gertrude in shocked tones. "You apologize to Cousin Allan at once! What an awful thing to say to anyone!"

"But it's true. He did say that."

"Nevertheless, you will apologize to your cousin," said Don firmly.

"I'm sorry I said that, Cousin Allan," said Roderick. But it really is true, and I'm not sorry, he thought. He stuck his lower lip out in a fierce pout.

"I guess I'd better get supper on," said Liz to change the subject. "The turkey's taking up half the pantry but it'll be thawed by morning."

"I'll go and open the doors upstairs so we won't need to be thawed in the morning," said Cassie. "Dear knows how long we'll be without power." She picked up the oil lamp and went upstairs. She began opening doors, and the light cast strange wavering shadows ahead of her as she moved through the hallway. A faint draft cooled her skin and she shivered.

This place isn't as air tight as that insulation man promised, she thought. Maybe we do need new windows.

She passed from room to room throwing the bedroom doors wide open. The faint outline of her figure with its bright spot of light from the lamp reflected in the windows and the mirrors as she went. I think I'll get a sweater while I'm up here, she thought.

She went into the room she shared with Liz and set the lamp on the dresser. A faint sound of wind chimes reached her ears. She looked up. Her reflection in the mirror wavered and faded before her eyes. It seemed as if someone else was standing there. She stood stalk still staring open-mouthed at the change in herself. The reflections moved and held out a beseeching hand to her before her own reflection reasserted itself and the vision faded.

Cassie shrieked and ran downstairs forgetting the sweater she'd gone in to get. The others piled out of the kitchen. Everyone talked at once. Liz got to her first.

"Whatever happened?" She put her arms around the hysterical Cassie.

Cassie babbled and tears flowed at full spate down her cheeks. "I saw, I saw, it was awful!" She waved her arms wildly trying to describe by pantomime what she had seen.

Liz led her into the kitchen and seated her

in the rocking chair which Aunt Maggie had vacated for what seemed to her like the dozenth time that day.

"What did you do with your lamp?" asked Liz gently.

Cassie gestured wildly in the direction of the upstairs. "I wouldn't, I wouldn't." She covered her face with her hands and began a fresh bout of sobbing.

"I'll go and get it," said Gertrude. "Where did you leave it?"

"Don't go, don't go by yourself." Cassie was beginning to recover some of her composure.

"Is there anything I can bring down for you? Your sweater perhaps?" Cassie was beginning to shiver noticeably.

"I'll go with you." Don set his book aside. Together he and Gertrude climbed the stairs.

"There's something up here alright," said Gertrude. "I can feel it."

Don groaned. "Every place we go there's always a ghost turns up. I wonder what the story is this time?"

"I don't know, but I'd sure like to find out. I wish Mary Ann and Big Jim were here. I sure could use some assistance from my colleagues right now."

"Well, they're not." Don's tone was short. "And I can't be of any help to you given my mortal limitations."

Gertrude entered Cassie's room and looked in the mirror. Her reflection was her own, although oddly changed by the shadows cast by the lamp. "Roderick may be of some help," she mused. "He's gained so much in sensitivity this past year I can hardly believe it."

Don sighed. "I was afraid it would come to this, although I didn't think it would be so soon. Are you sure he can handle it?"

It was Gertrude's turn to sigh. "I don't know." She began rummaging in the dresser drawer for Cassie's sweater. "At least there's Eddy and Freddy," she said of Roddy's guardians on the other side. "They can protect him psychically."

"Huh!" said Don, "the poker playing duo!

Some protection they are. I don't trust either one of them."

"Now Don, they'll do just fine. Especially if I sic Larry on them. I can always call Molly and Lucy, and if it really gets tough, maybe even Larry will come to help. Besides, I have my own guardians over there too." She picked up the lamp and headed out the door.

"What if Liz and Cassie don't want you to investigate?"

"They will," said Gertrude, "especially after what happened this evening."

Chapter Six

Cassie was much calmer but still shivering when Gertrude and Don returned to the kitchen. Gertrude placed the lamp on the table and draped Cassie's sweater around her shoulders. "There now, that should feel better."

"Thanks Gertrude, I couldn't have gone up there," she quavered. "You're very brave."

Gertrude shrugged. "Not really, I'm just my mother's daughter."

Aunt Maggie handed Cassie a cup of tea. "Here child, I put lots of sugar in it. You've had quite a shock. They say sugar's good for that. I remember when Murdoch got thrown from a horse in front of my very eyes. I was that shaky! It took me two cups of sweet tea to get me going again. Now, I'll tell you ..." She began to run on.

"I remember that," interrupted Uncle Will, who had been keeping out of the way most of the day. "That was when you two were first married. You were just a slip of a girl."

Aunt Maggie's blush was lost in the shadows. "Now, Will, you're embarrassing me." They both forgot that Maggie had weighed thirty pounds more in her youth and hadn't been a slip of a girl since she was eight.

Cassie drank her tea rapidly then held out her cup for a refill. Her shivering began to subside, and she was able to talk about her experience more lucidly. "I don't know what happened up there," she replied to Liz's question. "All I know is that there seemed to be someone else reflected in the mirror in our room. I heard the wind chimes too ... . At least I think I did."

"Who did the person in the mirror look like?" asked Gertrude.

"I don't know, it was superimposed over my own reflection and didn't really look like anyone."

"It was probably just the shadow from the lamp," said Aunt Maggie. "I remember one time I near scared myself to death with an oil lamp and it was all just shadows. Murdoch got such a fright when I screeched like a banshee and ran down the stairs. I tripped on the way down and fell the rest of the way, screeching all the way. It took poor Murdoch an hour to get me calmed down, God rest his soul." She sniffed at the memory.

"He was a good man," agreed Uncle Will, patting her hand. "A good man for a good woman." He smiled at Aunt Maggie making her blush again.

"Maybe it was Grand," suggested Allan. His upper lip curled slightly into a sneer. "He probably can't rest for having disinherited me."

"I know who it was, Mommy," said Roderick. He tugged at Gertrude's sleeve to get her attention. "It was Annie."

"Now, darling, I don't think that Annie would come back to this house, especially after all this time."

"But it was," insisted Roddy. "I know it was."

"That's enough, Roderick," said Don. "You mother's right, Annie wouldn't be coming back here. She was happy here, but she's dead now."

"That's what you think," muttered Roddy.

"I said, that's enough." Don's voice took on a harder edge.

Roddy's muttering subsided. He sat down on the floor beside Mr. Dog. "Nobody listens to me," he whispered to Mr. Dog. The faint sound of silver bells echoed again through the old farm house.

Cassie's teacup rattled in the saucer. She laughed feebly. "Maybe Roderick's right. Maybe it is Annie."

"Nonsense! This house has never been haunted, and I should know, I grew up here." Aunt Maggie firmed her lips at the very idea of a ghost inhabiting her childhood home, even if it was Annie's.

"I can vouch for that, agreed Uncle Will. "This has always been a very happy home. It was always a pleasure to come here."

"I think we should just have our supper and stop thinking about ghosts and hauntings," said Liz.

"We're letting our imaginations run away with us." She went into the pantry to fetch the dishcloth and the basket of cutlery. I hope I'm right, she thought. She remembered her own experience with the mirror. She gave herself a mental shake. I'll be as strange as Gertrude's mother if I keep this up. She returned to the kitchen. "Here Cassie, you can set the places. I'm going to slice some ham to go with the scalloped potatoes. Gertrude, would you check in the oven and see if they're done yet. They should be, they've been in plenty long."

Conversation at the supper table avoided the topic everyone really wanted to talk about.

Roderick's lip lost its pout by the time dessert was served.

"D'you want some Apple Brown Betty, Roderick?" asked Liz with the serving spoon in her hand. "It's good with real cream on it."

"I know," replied Roderick, "Annie just told me. It's her favourite." He held out his plate. "Just a little please, I don't have very much room left."

The spoon clattered out of Liz's hand and she sat down on her chair with a thump. "What did you just say?"

"I said, just a little, please."

"No, before that."

"Annie told me it was her favourite, she's here right now, you know."

Everyone looked around, nervously scanning the dark shadows cast by the oil lamps. Gertrude laughed apologetically. "He's got a vivid imagination, don't pay any attention to him."

"But Mommy, she's right there," protested Roderick, "and it's not right to tell lies."

Gertrude sighed and shook her head. "You or me this time, Don?"

"I will," said Don. He rose from his seat beside her and assisted Roderick to his feet with a firm hand beneath his elbow. "Come with me, young man. We're going to have a discussion about socially appropriate fictions and calling your mother a liar."

"But I didn't call Mommy a liar. I just meant that I can't tell a lie because it's not right." Tears were forming in Roderick's voice as the kitchen door was shut firmly behind him.

Dessert was finished in silence. Presently Uncle Will asked, "Is Grand's fiddle still here? I thought I might play a tune this evening."

"It's in its case under his bed, I think," said Liz. "It'll be great to hear some old tunes again." She began clearing the table. "Shall I save Roderick's pudding for him, Gertrude?"

"You'd better, he'll feel punished enough without missing dessert too."

Presently Gertrude and Liz were washing dishes in the pantry. "Trudy, I need to ask you something," said Liz. "Please don't be offended, and if you don't want to tell me, you can tell me to mind my own business."

"Gracious, this must be really serious." Gertrude laughed. "You even called me Trudy."

"It is serious." Liz kept her eyes on the soap bubbles she was making in the dish water with her hands. "Did your mother really have second sight?" She released the breath she hadn't realized she was holding.

Gertrude was silent for a moment. How do I answer that? she thought. "Why d'you want to know?"

Liz sighed. "I just thought you might have something to offer about what Cassie thought she saw upstairs this afternoon, you being Aunt Agnes' daughter."

"What makes you think that Cassie saw something besides shadows cast by the lamp?"

"Because I saw it one day too, in broad daylight."

"You did? When?"

"When we were here deciding on paper.

I didn't tell Cassie about it. I was afraid I'd frighten her and I wasn't real sure if it was me or the mirror."

"Was she there when you saw it?"

"Yes, she was sitting on the bed, and I was standing looking in the mirror."

"Hm," said Gertrude. "That is strange!"

"So did Aunt Agnes have the gift?"

"She liked to say she did, but I don't think she had very much. She used to make up a lot of stuff she told people, and she was pretty general, so it wasn't hard for them to find things coming true."

"Oh." Liz's tone was disappointed. "I was so hoping she had and that Roderick had inherited it."

Gertrude was aghast. "D'you mean you'd use my small son to go ghost hunting? Liz MacLean! Shame on you! He's only a baby yet."

Liz made a face. "Well, he talks like an adult, and besides, he's the one who keeps saying it's Annie. So I just thought, you know." She hitched her right shoulder as her voice trailed away. "I just thought that maybe he had the gift too, and could find out what Annie wanted, if it really is Annie." She subsided into a miserable silence.

"Liz, I'm going to share something with you, but before I do, I want your solemn promise that you won't breathe a word to any of the others." Gertrude looked at Liz with unwavering blue eyes.

"I-I promise." Liz's tone was doubtful.

"D'you really promise?" said Gertrude. She increased the intensity of her gaze.

Liz made up her mind. "Yes, I really promise, though I hope I don't live to regret this."

"This means no one," warned Gertrude.

"Not even Cassie?"

Gertrude sighed. "You may tell Cassie but not one other living soul."

Liz relaxed. "Good, I have a very hard time keeping things from Cassie, and I don't want to go against my word." She began washing dishes again. "So what is it that you want to share with me?"

"Well, I don't really want to share it, but I think I have to," said Gertrude. "You see, although Mom only had a very small gift, I have a big one, and Roderick has an even larger one."

Liz stopped washing dishes and turned to stare at Gertrude. "You do?! He does?"

"We do," said Gertrude firmly, "And I don't want it generally known. Life with Mom was misery enough for me. I don't want Roderick experiencing the same thing."

"Poor Don. What does he think of it?"

"He's learned to live with it."

Liz became aware of the water dripping from her fingers onto the floor. She turned back to washing dishes. "So do you think there's something here besides us?"

"Yes, I do. I've had the feeling ever since I came here that things are not quite right. I don't know what's triggered it, but something has. Maybe it's just this combination of people providing enough energy for the ghost to draw on."

"D'you suppose it could be Annie after all this time?"

"I don't know. Of course, it is possible, but why would she come back now? She's been gone, what, about twenty years?"

"Fifteen, although it seems longer." Liz sighed. "She was always so happy."

"What exactly happened to her? No one would ever tell me. I asked my mother once and she shut me up right quick, so I never asked again."

"She drowned. She went missing about supper time one evening and they just thought she'd gone off on one of her rambles, and forgotten the time. They got worried when she hadn't reappeared by bedtime and they went looking for her. They found her body floating in the brook down by the bridge in the lane. It's pretty deep there, and we were always warned to stay away from it."

"How'd they find her in the dark?"

"They only had lamps and a few feeble flashlights. She couldn't answer them when they called so they had to rely on seeing her, or that she would make some noise to attract their attention. I think it was Allan who found her. There was a little skiff of snow on the ground and he followed her footsteps." Liz wrung out the dishcloth and began wiping the counter.

"Oh, yes, I remember now, she couldn't talk, could she?"

"No, she could make some soft sounds." Liz thought back to their childhood. "Early on she spoke well for her age, but all of a sudden, when she was about six or seven, she just stopped and nobody could figure out why. She had been out here with Grand and Aunt Lizzie for a week. Will lived here then. Allan was just a little fellow."

"I wonder why that was?"

"I don't know. Our parents took her to hospitals and clinics all over the place and no one could find out the answer. Mom said one time that she'd had a hard time delivering her, and that the doctors likened her condition to a stroke where she understands everything, but can't form words to reply. They finally put it down to brain damage at birth."

"She went to school, didn't she?"

"After the first couple of grades she just came with us and I suppose she learned. The teachers could never tell because she couldn't write or answer questions on exams. In those days there weren't all the itinerant teachers and fancy programs to help people like her." Liz began stacking the dried dishes in the cupboard.

"How long did she go to school for?" Gertrude handed Liz the stack of dinner plates.

"It seems to me she went until she was fourteen. I don't really remember. I was about eleven when she stopped coming with us. She was very sweet and beautiful and trusting, and the boys started teasing her about her looks and her figure. When Mom found out about it, she took her out of school. I guess she feared the worst."

Gertrude laughed wryly. "Don't they

always! I remember my mother warning me about the boys in the darkest tones. She never came right out and said what it was they might do, but then she started in on the Catholic boys and how I shouldn't date them, and I thought for the longest time that it was the Catholic boys who made you pregnant. Not that I ever had too much to do with the Catholic boys, nor with the Protestant boys either for that matter."

Liz shook her head and laughed too. "It's a wonder we weren't afraid to go out the lane!" She gave a final wipe to the counter just as Uncle Will began tuning up Grand's old violin.

"Oh good, you're going to play for us," said Cassie. "Can you play 'Big John McNeil'?"

"Aye, that's a good one, but you'll have to wait until I get my fingers warmed up. It takes a bit of dexterity to play that one." He turned the tuning pegs and fussed with the fine tuner.

"Hand me the rosin, like a good girl, please. This bow is pretty dry after all these months."

Cassie handed him the rosin. "Gold! That's pretty fancy stuff."

"Grand was a master at this; he always had the best." Uncle Will tried the fiddle for tune one last time, then slipped into the opening notes of 'Westphalia Waltz.' He followed this with 'Ragtime Annie,' and then 'St. Annie's Reel.' Everyone's toes were tapping, and Roderick turned circles in the middle of the floor until he was dizzy. "Are you ready now, Cassie? Here's your tune." He launched into the spirited tune, 'Big John McNeil.'

Tune after tune poured out from the old fiddle that evening. Stories were told with much laughter. Allan sat in the shadows on the lounge and scowled. The others ignored him. "We should sing some Christmas carols," suggested Aunt Maggie, "after all, it is Christmas Eve."

They sang every carol they knew until finally Uncle Will called a halt. "My fingers have had it," he said. "I haven't played this much in a year."

"Push the kettle over on the fire would you, Gertrude, you're handy. We'll have a cup of tea," said Liz.

"D'you suppose Santa will find me here?" asked Roderick when he was getting ready for bed awhile later.

"I think so," replied Gertrude. "He always finds you at Uncle Jim's, doesn't he?"

"We were only there once, and I told him in my letter where I'd be." He began buttoning his pyjama tops. "Mommy, can I tell you something?"

"Of course, darling, what is it?"

"You won't get mad at me will you?"

"No."

"Well, Daddy said that just because I know things to be true, that it doesn't mean that everyone else does too."

"That's right," said Gertrude. "Why are you

thinking about that now?"

"I've been thinking about it all evening because it doesn't make sense."

"Why doesn't it make sense?"

"Because Annie was there all evening and there was a man there too, and they were singing and clapping time to Uncle Will's music, but nobody paid them any attention. It was like they weren't even there."

Gertrude sighed, then gathered Roderick onto her lap. "Honey, not everyone can see what you and I see. We have a very special gift, but it must be kept secret. Not everyone would understand about it, and it scares people who don't understand. That's why you and I have to be careful what we say in front of people. We don't want frighten them away. That would be very unkind." Gertrude thought back to her dysfunctional childhood and sighed again.

Roderick rolled off Gertrude's lap and onto the bed. He began pulling on his bed socks. "Does it make you unhappy?"

"Not anymore. I've come to realize how important it is, and how I can help people with it."

"Can Daddy see what we see?"

"No, Daddy can't see what we see, but he believes that we see it, so it's not a problem for him. C'mon now, hop into bed and get warm." She lifted the covers and Roderick climbed into the cot.

"Did you see Annie this evening?" Roderick snuggled deeper under the blankets.

"I wasn't looking," said Gertrude. "You forgot to say your prayers."

"Can I say them here, it's cold out there."

"I guess God won't mind." Gertrude smiled down at her son and thought, I'm glad that part of the explanation's over with. She listened to Roderick's childish 'now I lay me down to sleep.'

"You know, Annie wants to tell us something," said Roderick when he'd finished his prayers. He regarded his mother with serious blue eyes.

"And what's that?"

"I don't know, she can't say it out loud."

"Can she say it in your mind?"

Roderick concentrated for a moment. "No, she says I'm too little to know about things like that."

"Well, then don't worry about it. You go to sleep and Daddy and I'll be up in a little while."

CHAPTER SEVEN

The household was awakened that night by the sound of a hoarse male shout followed by scrambling footsteps and a slamming door. Gertrude's feet hit the cold floor before she was fully awake. The icy shock brought her rapidly to full awareness. She hastily stuck her feet into her slippers, grabbed her flashlight and hurried out the door.

She found Allan curled into a protective ball cowering in the corner of the hallway with his knees drawn up to his chest and his hands held out beseechingly to an unseen threat. "No-o, no, don't," he moaned. He covered his face with his hands. "Get away from me!"

Gertrude reached him as the others came out of their rooms. "Allan! Allan! Stop it!" She shook him firmly by the shoulders. "Wake up!"

Allan uncovered his face slowly and looked out at the others through half-closed eyelids. Embarrassment turned his swarthy complexion a dull red. "What're you all staring at?" he almost snarled. He buried his face in his hands again to shut out the sight of them.

"C'mon Allan," said Gertrude, "let me help you up. Was it a nightmare you had?"

Allan rolled to his knees and got to his feet. "Yes," he snapped, "and I'd like all of you to stop staring at me."

Gertrude put her hand on his arm. "Why don't you come downstairs with me and I'll make you a nice hot drink. Some cambric tea, perhaps. It'll help you go back to sleep."

Allan shook her roughly away. "I don't want any cambric tea, Miss Priss. Just leave me alone."

"Something stronger then," persisted Gertrude.

"Well, maybe," Allan growled, and stomped off downstairs in the dark. "Ow!" echoed from the darkness below as he collided with the sharp end of the rocking chair. "Damn! Why'd I come here anyway?"

"I guess I'd better get down there and light the lamp before he breaks a leg," said Gertrude with a wry grin. "I'll see if I can calm him down, you guys go back to bed." She headed downstairs after Allan.

"What was the dream all about, Allan?" Gertrude struck a match and applied it to the wick of the oil lamp.

"None of your business," he replied. "You'll only tell the others."

"No, I won't. Not if you don't want me to."

"Oh, yes, now I remember! The ever virtuous Trudy. Always keeps her promises."

"I try," said Gertrude. "It'll help if you talk about it, you know."

Allan's shoulders slumped. "I dreamed about Annie."

"I see. Can you elaborate on that a little?" Gertrude went into the pantry to get a saucepan and the milk while Allan thought it over.

"I dreamed she was coming for me, and was going to take me with her to Grand. She kept coming toward me with her hand out and a smile on her face. She didn't say a word."

"Well, that's not surprising." Gertrude stirred up the remnants of last night's fire and set the milk over the hole to heat. "She couldn't talk when she was alive, so you'd have no way of knowing what she'd sound like if she did say anything." The sound of her spoon scraping the edges of the pan filled the kitchen as Allan thought about this. The wind whistled around the eaves as the last of the storm blew itself out.

"I suppose you're right." He lapsed into silence. After a few moments he said on the end of a sigh, "She was lovely."

"She was that." Gertrude handed him his

warm milk. "Do you dream about her often?"

"No." Allan took a sip from his mug. "At least not until Grand died." He took another sip from his mug. "You don't know if there's any of Grand's 'medicine' left in the pantry, do you?"

"I dunno, I'll look." Gertrude rose and went to rummage in the pantry cupboard. "There's a little." She tipped the bottle to its corner. "I don't know how long it's been there, I guess that stuff doesn't spoil." She poured a generous serving into Allan's mug.

"Thanks," said Allan. "How'd you turn out so nice?"

Gertrude shrugged. "Don."

"He seems like a good man." Allan stared into his mug for a few seconds before draining it. "I wish I could be a good man."

"Aren't you?"

"Not according to some people." He got to his feet. "Thanks, Trudy. I'll see you in the morning."

§

Christmas morning dawned clear and bright. The wind lifted swirls of sparkling snow and banked it against the house and barns. Nothing else moved in the shining blue and white world except the ravens behind the house. They called raucously to one another and fought over the meagre opportunities for winter food.

Roderick ran from window to window where he'd melted little peek holes through the frost. "Look, Mommy, look! The snow is up to the window sills. Can I go out and play in it?"

"Not by yourself, you can't," said Gertrude, "and not until after breakfast. Besides, don't you want to see what Santa brought you?"

"Oh, I forgot about him." Roderick ran to the mantle shelf and stood on tiptoes to take down his bulging stocking.

"I guess it's a good job we did leave the cars

at the road," said Uncle Will. He bent to peer out the hole in the frost that Roderick had made on the window pane. "It'll be spring before this'll melt."

Cassie and Liz exchanged glances. "We just want to be sure you wouldn't be stuck here against your will," punned Cassie.

"Grand has a snow blower in the barn," said Allan. "I can take a little gas from my truck and clear around the door."

"That'd be nice," said Liz. "I don't think we can even open the door now, never mind get across the yard."

Allan shrugged. "The back door will be drifted clear, it always is."

"You're certainly chipper this morning after keeping us up half the night," said Uncle Will. "What was it, a nightmare or something you ate?"

"Something I ate," snapped Allan. "Not that it's any of your affair."

Will ignored Allan's attempt at dismissing the subject. "You used to have them a lot growing up. You used to pee the bed and everything when you'd have one."

Allan's face took on a closed angry look. Liz rushed to his defence. "He was only a child then, Uncle Will."

"Oh, no. This was when he was a teenager. They started right after Annie drowned."

"Shut up, you stupid old man! Just shut up! You don't know the first thing about it!" Allan shook his fist at his uncle.

"Don't I just," persisted Will with a sly glance at Liz. "There's a lot of things I could be telling but I'm not."

Allan clamped his lips shut and stomped out of the kitchen. Presently they heard the porch door slam and a few minutes later the sound of the snow blower started up.

Liz sighed. "Now why'd you have to pick on him like that, Uncle Will? It's a fine way to start Christmas day." She frowned at Will on her way to the pantry to collect the cutlery for the table.

"Yes, Will, why'd you have to go and do

that?" asked Aunt Maggie. "You know he's always short in the grain when we're all here together."

Uncle Will chuckled. "It'll teach him some restraint."

"Maybe some manners too. Imagine talking to you like that!" She clucked her tongue at the idea.

The lights flickered and then stayed on as electricity was restored to the Island. The furnace started immediately, and the water heater behind the kitchen stove creaked into life.

"Good, we'll have lots of hot water in a few minutes," said Liz.

"And lights for the Christmas tree while we open our presents," said Cassie.

"I'm going to turn on the T.V. and see what the weather forecast is." Don headed into the parlour. In a few minutes he returned. "There's another big one on the way. It'll be here by tonight. They're expecting another thirty to forty-five centimetres, depending where it hits."

"Oh, boy!" shouted Roderick. "The snow'll be up to the roof!"

Gertrude and Don exchanged glances. "Well, I guess we won't be getting home tomorrow," she said. "By the time we get the car shovelled out and a hole cut in the bank to drive through, the storm'll be upon us again."

"The plow hasn't been through yet, either," Allan reported, coming in from outdoors, his civility restored. "I rode the snowmobile up to the road to have a look and it isn't even in sight."

"We may be in for a long siege of it," said Liz handing Allan a cup of tea. "Thanks for doing all that work."

"Much good it may do us," said Allan. "The wind blows it back almost as fast as I could blow it out."

"We'll be all right. There's plenty to eat and we're warm and dry. What else could we need?" said Liz. A soft tinkle of wind chimes followed her words.

"Annie's here," said Roderick so softly only

Gertrude heard.

"Ssh, ssh," she warned quietly.

"There's them wind chimes again," observed Aunt Maggie. She began to rock more vigorously. "I'd sure like to know what Grand was doing with them things."

"Oh, ho, so we're back to Annie again, are we?" said Will.

Allan didn't reply.

"Let's go in and see what Santa's brought us." Liz led the way into the parlour. "Who wants to play Santa?"

"I will," said Cassie copying Liz's tone of voice. "Roderick can be an elf and pass things around."

Everyone was well pleased with their gifts and by mid-afternoon they sat down to roast turkey, its skin crisply brown, fluffy mashed potatoes, carrots, fried parsnips and mashed turnips, all smothered in brown turkey gravy with lots of onions. Bread crumb dressing seasoned with summer savoury and minced onion completed the main course. Lady Ross relish and whole cranberry sauce provided tart sweet highlights to the meal.

"Seconds, anyone?" offered Liz. "Remember there's still dessert to go."

"I could handle a little more potatoes and gravy," said Aunt Maggie. She held out her plate. "That turkey was awful good, nice and moist. How'd you keep it like that?"

"I roasted it covered, with lots of water on it," said Liz. "I only took the cover off for the last hour to brown it." She handed Aunt Maggie's plate back to her, laden with a little of everything. "I made the gravy out of the juice that was left."

"Well, you do your mother proud," said Will. "She was a wonderful cook, and that was a feast fit for a king."

"Why, thank you, Uncle Will," said Liz. "I hope you've left room for some plum pudding and brown sugar sauce."

He patted his stomach. "I think I can find a little space somewhere."

The day darkened early as the approaching

storm clouded the sky. Allan and Don had taken Roderick out for a romp in the snow after dinner. A ride on the snowmobile with cousin Allan completed the excitement for him.

"Cousin Allan took me for a ride on the snowmobile, Mommy." Roderick fairly bounced on the porch floor. "All the way up to the road to see if the plow had come. D'you know the cars are buried all the way up to their roofs." He paused for breath.

"And did the plow come through?" Gertrude began peeling layers of wet scarf from around Roderick's rosy face.

"It was a big snow blower and it blew the snow higher than the power lines! It just went whoosh and covered everything up." Roderick windmilled his arms to demonstrate.

Gertrude unzipped Roderick's jacket and pulled off his wet mittens. "Did you and Daddy and Allan make a snowman like you planned?"

"No, we tried, but the snow was too soft." Roderick sat down on the floor with a thump and began pulling his boots off. "We couldn't get it to stick together. Cousin Allan said we'd have to wait 'til spring to get sticky snow, but we won't be here in the spring, will we?"

"No, honey, probably not, but you can make a snowman at home in the backyard." Gertrude knelt down to help him pull off his snow pants and heavy socks. "If you behave real good, maybe Liz and Cassie'll invite you back to make a snowman in the spring."

Roderick scrambled to his feet. "Oh, boy! I'm going to ask Liz if we can come back if I'm good." He hurried off in search of Liz and Cassie.

Liz and Cassie were sitting in the parlour on the floor rearranging the presents under the tree. Christmas carols played softly over CFCY radio. Occasional gusts of wind sent drifting snow hissing against the window. They were so deep in conversation they didn't notice.

"D'you suppose it really is Annie?" asked

Cassie refolding the sweater she'd gotten from Liz.

Liz pursed her lips thoughtfully. "I don't know any better than you do, Cassie. I can only speculate." She reached to turn the tree lights on.

"If it is Annie, why'd she come back now? Why not years ago? Why not right after she drowned?"

Liz shrugged. "How should I know? Actually, Gertrude had a good suggestion last night. She said that it may be because of the make up of this particular group of people. That Annie is able to draw on the power of this group better than when just Grand was here."

The gathering storm had slowly darkened the room and the tree lights cast a soft glow on Cassie's creamy skin. She leaned her elbows on her knees while she considered this. "How does Gertrude know so much about it?"

"She's got the gift," said Liz flatly, "and so does Roderick."

"She does?! They do?! So that's why they shut Roderick up so quick last night when he was talking about Annie. Maybe Annie really was here and we just couldn't see her. I guess she gets it from her mother, eh?"

"No, she said her mother didn't have much of the gift, that she made most of that stuff up when she read for people. Now you mustn't tell anyone. Gertrude swore me to secrecy because of Roderick."

"So why're you telling me?" asked Cassie.

"She said I could tell you, but that neither one of us was to tell. She said she had a miserable childhood because of how her mother behaved, and she didn't want that for Roderick. Okay?"

"Okay." Cassie fell silent for a moment, then said, "So will she help us find out what Annie wants?"

"I don't know, I didn't ask her that," said Liz. "I guess I was having too hard a time taking in that she really does have the gift, I didn't think of its possible uses."

"I wonder if it's us that Annie wants to contact?" A faint sound of wind chimes floated through the air and mingled with the carols on the radio, but the two girls didn't hear.

The evening had been filled with music from Grand's old fiddle and stories from long ago. "Mommy, Mommy, Annie's here again." Roderick tugged at his mother's sweater sleeve. "That old man is with her." His loud whisper was heard by everyone. Talk ceased for a moment while they all craned their heads to see into the darker corners of the room.

Gertrude laughed nervously. "Sorry folks, his imagination's on the loose again. I think it's time he was in bed."

Everyone relaxed and Will tuned up the fiddle for 'Smash the Window' jig and 'Soldier's Joy.'

"D'you want something to eat before you go up to bed, Roderick?"

"Can't I please stay up, Mommy? Please?

Please?" Roderick looked pleadingly at his mother. "I'll be good."

"No more talk of Annie?"

"Not even to you?"

"Not in front of others. We can talk when you go up to bed. Now remember, you promised. No more talk of Annie."

"I promise."

"Okay, you can stay up a little while longer." Gertrude turned her attention to the music. I must try and have a chat with Annie, she thought, that is, if she can speak in the ethereal.

The lights went out so abruptly that everyone was startled. "Well, that was certainly sudden," said Liz. She fumbled on the shelf for a flashlight. Her hand passed through a cold spot and she jumped back knocking the flashlight to the floor. It rolled away from her grasp. "Open the stove lid so I can see what I'm doing, please."

Cassie jumped to her feet to assist Liz. As she lifted the lid she glanced up to the warming oven on top of the stove. What she saw made her gasp. She dropped the stove lid with a crash, plunging the kitchen into nearly total darkness again. She backed away from the stove, pointing and gesturing speechlessly at the warming oven. In the darkness no one could see her. She kept backing up until she fetched up against Uncle Will's knees and collapsed on his lap, narrowly missing the violin.

"Well, now, isn't this nice," said Uncle Will who hadn't seen what Cassie had seen. He patted her cheek and tweaked her bottom at the same time.

Cassie rose from his lap with a shriek. The apparition on the warming oven seemed to laugh. Cassie yelled, "Get him!" as she rubbed her offended bottom.

Everyone thought she meant Uncle Will and Allan and Don leaped to restrain him as he reached out to assist Cassie in soothing her bruised anatomy.

"Not him! Him!" She pointed in the direction of the warming oven.

Liz managed to lift the stove lid again and

found the oil lamp and matches to light the lamp. As the glow from the wick increased and steadied, the figure on the warming oven faded. A fierce gust of wind shook the house.

"It was Grand! Why didn't you catch him?" babbled Cassie still rubbing her bottom.

"Grand! Where was he?" Liz raised the lamp higher to cast more light.

"Sitting on the warming oven," said Cassie. "I saw him right there." She pointed again at the stove.

"Pretty warm up there, even for the likes of Grand, isn't it?" said Aunt Maggie. She hadn't seen a thing either and probably never would. "I think you're seeing things, Cassie. Being shut up here in the dead of winter is enough to drive anyone crazy. Why, I remember Murdoch telling me about old Peter down in Primrose, the winter they had so much snow. He lived by himself and got snowed in and he was a 'ravening' lunatic by spring!" Aunt Maggie rambled on, and no one paid her any heed.

"He was a raving lunatic anyway" said Uncle Will in the background.

"I think I'll put the kettle on," said Liz. "A cup of tea may calm us down." She added another stick to the fire and pushed the kettle over the firebox to get hot. "A bite to eat might not come amiss either. Gertrude, can you help me in the pantry?"

Gertrude rose and followed Liz into the pantry.

Liz closed the door behind them. "Did you see anything?" she demanded.

"No, I was too busy trying to keep Roderick quiet. He was going on about Annie being here and a man being with her. I didn't want him announcing his gift to the whole world, especially to Aunt Maggie. She'd have the news all over Charlottetown in jig time."

Cassie squeezed into the small pantry with them. "I saw Grand as plain as day, sitting on top of the warming oven. He actually laughed when Uncle Will pinched me!"

"Is that what happened? I thought you were

going to have a fit right there," chuckled Liz. "Well, Grand always did get a kick out of Uncle Will's shenanigans with the girls."

"Some shenanigans! That hurt!" Cassie rubbed her bottom again.

"Did you see Annie too?" asked Gertrude. "Roddy said they were both there."

"No, I was too taken with seeing Grand. Did you see anything, Liz?"

"No, but I sure felt it. I put my hand through a cold spot and it scared me. That's when I dropped the flashlight." She began slicing bread. "What are we going to do about it?" She stacked the bread on a plate. "Can you help us, Trudy?"

"I can try," said Gertrude, "though I've only seen Annie once or twice when I was little, and I only remember how Grand looked in his coffin."

"Will a photograph help? There are plenty of those in the parlour."

"It's a place to start, but it'll have to wait until morning when we'll have some decent light. In the meantime, I think we'd better get some food on the table. The natives are getting restless out there. I can hear Uncle Will winding up to start picking on Allan again."

"Why does he have to do that?" moaned Liz. "He knows Allan has a short temper."

Cassie sighed. "That's probably why."

Chapter Eight

The wind complained loudly in the eaves all night. Snow hissed softly against the frosted window panes and found its way in past ill-fitting sashes. A particularly forceful gust woke Gertrude at two o'clock and she lay for some time listening to the ebb and flow of the storm.

I might as well get up and make myself something warm to drink, she thought. I'll not be getting to sleep anymore tonight if I don't. She rolled out of bed being careful not to wake Don and stuck her feet into her fluffy slippers. Feeling around the foot of the bed in the dark she found her robe and pulled it on. She felt for her flashlight and managed to find it without knocking it over, then crept downstairs.

She was startled to see a shadowy figure in the rocking chair. "Is that you, Annie?" she asked softly.

"No, it's me," said Liz. "Can't you sleep either?"

"No, the storm woke me, I came down to get something to drink."

"I just put some more wood on the stove, so it should get nice and warm in here pretty soon. Can I get you anything?"

"No, thanks, I'll help myself." Gertrude went into the pantry. Presently she came back with a saucepan and two mugs. "I found some cocoa on the the shelf. I thought you might like some if I made it."

"Thanks," said Liz, "That does sound good." She sat silently for some minutes staring at the firelight flickering through the draft in the side of the stove. Then she said, "What'll you do to contact Annie?"

"Trance, I guess." Gertrude stirred the milk continuously with the wooden spoon. "It's the most effective way usually."

"You can do that?"

"It's my work."

"Your work? Who do you work for?"

"Have you ever heard of Jim MacDonald?"

"The guy who lives in Cherry Valley in that house with all the antennas sticking out of his roof?"

"That's the one." Gertrude tested the cocoa on the edge of her lip, deemed it ready and began pouring it into the mugs.

"They say he's kind of strange," said Liz. "I heard that he plants his garden by the phases of the moon and leaves offerings for the fairies!"

Gertrude laughed softly. "That's him, and he has the lushest garden on the Island too."

"How'd you come to be working for him?"

"He was a friend of Don's from college days, and when I went to see Don regarding some of the strange experiences I was having, he suggested that I might like to meet with Jim and Mary Ann."

"Is Mary Ann his wife?"

"No, she's just a neighbour and friend. She's also a sensitive, and before I discovered my abilities she used to do a lot of the psychic work for him. She still does. We work together on cases."

"So how'd you discover your psychic abilities?"

"D'you remember Molly MacIntosh?"

"I remember her name. Wasn't she that old woman who used to clean houses for everyone who was anyone in Charlottetown? She used to tell fortunes on the side, someone said."

Gertrude nodded. "That's her. She was a sensitive too, most of her life. She had a stroke and ended up in the nursing home where I worked. She and I struck sparks off each other every time we met. She couldn't talk very well anymore because of the stroke. She used to substitute words, and the more agitated she became, the worse it got. Anyway, she had a couple of otherworldly pals who taught her how to exit her body whenever she wanted to, and she and they decided it was time that I acknowledged my gift. They did the worst things to me, and I resisted all the way because I didn't want to be like my mother. Everyone just thought she was crazy. That's when I met up with Don again. I went to consult about the problems I was having. I was convinced that I was as strange as my mother ever tried to be. He tested me every way he could think of and analyzed me to atoms and finally had to admit defeat. He said that the only other thing to do was to accept for the moment that what was happening to me was real and not just an overactive imagination and burnout. I'd been working twelve hour shifts and using all that time off to work a second job to pay for Mom's nursing home down in Texas, so I was worn out. He introduced me to Jim and Mary Ann, and here we are six years later."

Liz laughed. "Snowed in with some

questionable people and a couple of ghosts."

"It could be worse, you know."

A hoarse cry from upstairs brought both Liz and Gertrude to their feet. "That sounds like Uncle Will!" said Liz. She set her mug down and grabbed the flashlight and ran up the stairs two at a time. Gertrude was close behind. They arrived at the top of the stairs in time to see Uncle Will being dragged, kicking and struggling from his room by his feet. The only thing visible was a strange glow around his ankles.

"Stop that at once!" shouted Gertrude. The light wavered and then disappeared. Uncle Will's heels hit the hardwood floor with a thump and he scrambled to his feet.

"Are you alright?" asked Liz. She began brushing dust bunnies from Will's long johns.

"No, I am not alright!" said Uncle Will. "What kind of house are you running here anyway?" He was shaking so much that it was difficult to understand what he was saying, especially without his teeth.

"Let me help you back to bed," said Liz. She took his arm.

Will shook her off. "I'm not going to sleep in that bed again, and if I could, I'd go home right now. Things like that never happened when Grand was alive."

"That's why," said Allan from the shadows of the doorway where he'd been quietly taking in the scene.

"Just what do you mean by that?" demanded Uncle Will.

"You know what I mean," said Allan. "It couldn't happen when Grand was alive because he didn't know." He turned on his heel and went back into the room. "Here's your pants, Will, you'd better put them on." The pants came flying through the door and wrapped themselves around Aunt Maggie's curlered head just as she stuck it out of her bedroom door to see what was happening.

"What's going on out here?" She yanked a denim pant leg and a few curlers off her head. "Will, put your pants on! You should be ashamed, parading around like that in front of these young women!"

Gertrude and Liz began to giggle. "It's alright Aunt Maggie, we've seen worse."

"Indeed!" Aunt Maggie was momentarily speechless. She turned and flounced back into her room without ever finding out what she wanted to know. "Things like this never went on in my day!" She slammed the door.

Liz and Gertrude went back downstairs. "What d'you suppose that was all about?" asked Liz. "Did you see anything?"

"Just that glow," said Gertrude.

"But you spoke to it."

Gertrude shrugged. "I assumed there was an intelligence behind it, since it couldn't have done what it was doing if there wasn't. So I just shouted at it. It never did reveal its identity."

"I wonder why it picked on Uncle Will?"

"Dear knows." Gertrude laughed. "Maybe it

was after Allan and couldn't see in the dark."
She sipped at her remaining cocoa. "Yuck,
that's cold now." She set the mug back on
the table. "I think I'll go back up and see if
I can get some sleep yet tonight. It's already
nearly five." The faint sound of bells followed
her upstairs.

"My back hurts," grumbled Uncle Will at
breakfast the next morning.

"It's no wonder, the tricks you were up
to last night!" said Aunt Maggie. "Such
goings on I never did see. What were you
doing anyway?"

"I had a nightmare," mumbled Will.

"What was that you said?" gibed Allan from
his place on the lounge. "And did you pee
the bed?"

"You just shut your mouth," snapped Will.

"Oh, I see, it's okay if you say it to me, but
not if I say it to you."

"Mind your own business!"

"Let me guess, you had a dream about Annie and Grand, didn't you?"

Will's face took on a purplish cast as he searched for a fitting retort.

"Allan! Cut it out!" said Cassie.

"Okay, but you'll see." He went back to reading last year's issue of *Island Company*, a smile of triumph still curling the corners of his lips.

"We're going to have to talk to that Allan," said Liz. She and Gertrude were washing dishes in the pantry. "I don't see what he's up to, but whatever it is, he nearly gave Uncle Will a stroke when he made that crack about the dream."

"He's been acting strange ever since Grand died," said Cassie. She had squeezed into the pantry and was trying to help put things away. "He keeps hinting at things and never saying them and it's very annoying."

"Well, you know Allan," said Gertrude.

"He's been like that ever since he was a little fellow. He always wanted us to think he had a secret." She handed a stack of dried plates to Cassie.

"I know," said Liz, "but he was never this bad. As a matter of fact, I don't think this all started until after Annie died. He was always kind of horrible in a little boy sort of way, but now he's downright malicious."

"And it all seems to be directed at Uncle Will," said Gertrude.

"I think he's just mad because of Grand's will," said Cassie. "I think he expected to inherit and was really disappointed when he didn't."

"And rightfully so," said Liz. "He was Grand's son in fact, if not in deed. He should have inherited." She began mopping up the counter with the dishcloth.

"I wonder why he didn't?" Gertrude passed the last stack of dried dishes to Cassie.

"I don't know," replied Liz, "and I'm not sure if Allan even knows."

"I'll bet he does," said Cassie. She closed the cupboard doors with a click. "I'll bet he and Grand had a falling out before he went away to work in Fredricton."

"Maybe." Liz shrugged. "Whatever's stuck in his craw's giving him indigestion."

"Well, we invited everyone here this year to try to heal the family wounds," said Cassie, "and as far as I can tell, they're only getting worse." The faint tinkle of wind chimes followed her words. "There're those darned bells again! They're getting on my nerves!"

"I think that's Annie agreeing with us," chuckled Gertrude, only half seriously.

The day wore endlessly on. The storm continued to beat against the house with varying intensity. The snow drifted higher and higher. No one talked much. Gertrude could feel the tension of the group rising with the snow drifts. I wish this storm would quit so we could get out of here, she thought. I don't think it's good for Roderick to be cooped up here with all the bad feelings that are circulating. As a matter of fact, I think I'll try and contact Annie myself and see if she'll tell me what she wants.

Gertrude went into the parlour and closed the door. At least it's warm in here, she thought. She put another stick in the pot-bellied stove, then settled herself in Grand's armchair and closed her eyes. Relaxation didn't come easily. The presence of the others in the kitchen across the hall interfered with her ability to concentrate. I wish Mary Ann was here, she thought. She could keep watch for me. She took a deep cleansing breath, visualizing her anxious thoughts going out of her with its exhalation.

"Annie, Annie," she called in her mind. The image of a young girl with strawberry blond curls floated into her awareness. "Is that you, Annie?"

The image smiled and nodded.

"What do you need from us here, Annie?"

The girl's lips moved but no sound came

forth. An expression of distress crossed her lovely features. Her blue eyes filled with tears.

"I can't hear you, Annie. Can you say that again?"

Annie's lips moved again, and again there was no sound. She held out her hand beseechingly to Gertrude and faded from Gertrude's awareness.

"It's alright, Annie," called Gertrude softly in her mind. "I'll find someone to help us." She turned her internal attention to her colleague on the other side. "Molly! Molly!" she called. "Come here, I need you."

"I'm coming! I'm coming! Keep your shirt on," snapped Molly from her perch on top of the Christmas tree. "What do you want in such a hurry?"

Gertrude laughed at the sight of the turbaned Molly as a tree top ornament. "I need some information."

"Don't you always," said Molly. "What is it this time?"

"What d'you know about Annie MacLean?"

"D'you mean butterfly Annie? The one that's always picking daisies?"

"I guess that's who I mean," said Gertrude. "She's a sister to Liz and Cassie who've just inherited this house, and she keeps dropping in unexpectedly. She was just here a minute ago."

Molly shrugged. "Not much. She can't talk, but for the life of me I can't understand why. Somebody said it was because of an earth trauma years ago."

"Shouldn't that have been repaired when she took her therapeutic sleep when she first came over?"

"It should have been, but she wouldn't, or couldn't sleep, so it didn't repair itself."

"I wonder what it could have been, to have had such a profound effect on her?"

"Dunno," said Molly. "Look, if that's all you wanted to ask me, I have to go." She began to fade from Gertrude's awareness.

"Find out what she wants, if you can, and let me know," called Gertrude after Molly's disappearing form.

Drat! thought Gertrude. I hope she heard me. She has no more patience now than when she was in the physical.

The parlour door opened and Liz came in carrying an armload of wood for the fire. "Oops, sorry, I didn't know you were napping in here."

"I wasn't." Gertrude sat up and rubbed her eyes. "I was trying to contact Annie."

"Oh, double sorry," said Liz, "I hope I didn't disturb you at a crucial moment." She dropped the short logs into the woodbox with a thump.

Gertrude yawned. "No, I was just coming back."

"Did you talk to Annie?"

"I tried, she can't talk. She wanted to, but she just couldn't do it."

"She couldn't talk when she was here either, so maybe that's no surprise."

"She should have recovered her power of speech over there, though. I asked Molly about it, and she said that she didn't know why she hadn't."

"What else did Molly say?"

"Not much. I asked her to find out for me, but I don't know if she heard me."

Chapter Nine

The light waned as the sun set unseen behind the thick clouds. Liz lighted the lamp and set it on the kitchen table. "I'd start supper if I thought anyone was hungry," she said. No one spoke. Liz shrugged and went back to her book. Aunt Maggie rocked on in the rocking chair before the stove. She was silent for once. Her knitting needles clicked industriously. Allan dozed on the lounge. Roderick sat on the floor by Mr. Dog and played with his trucks. Uncle Will and Don talked politics on the other side of the stove. Uncle Will's rocking chair rocked harder and faster the more emotional energy he put into his argument. Cassie and Gertrude played Auction at the table. Presently Gertrude felt a tug at her sweater sleeve. She bent over to hear what Roddy wanted.

"They're coming soon," whispered Roddy.

"Who's coming, darling?"

"Annie and Grand. They'll be here this evening."

"That's not so unusual, they were here yesterday evening too," said Gertrude. She went back to her game.

"Mommy!" Roderick tugged at her sleeve again. "Annie told me in my mind that Grand was going to fix things this evening."

"What things?" Roderick had her full attention now.

Roderick shrugged. "I don't know, she didn't tell me."

"I guess we'll find out in due time," said Gertrude.

"I guess so." Roderick turned and wandered somewhat aimlessly back to his trucks and

Mr. Dog. "Well, I told her, Mr. Dog." He began making truck noises again.

"Anyone for a game of Hearts?" asked Cassie after supper. "It'll help pass the time."

"Not me," said Allan. "The wind's died down. I think I'll blow out this end of the lane." He pulled on his overshoes and shrugged into his down jacket.

"Don't fall into the brook," said Uncle Will with a nasty edge to his voice.

Allan chose not to answer in favour of slamming the door behind himself.

"That lad's got a nasty temper," said Uncle Will. "It'll get him in trouble some day."

"That it will," agreed Aunt Maggie.

"He's only crabby when you're at him," said Cassie.

"Mind your manners, miss," said Aunt Maggie. "You shouldn't speak to your uncle like that!"

Cassie sighed and looked at Liz.

"More tea anyone? I just made a fresh pot." Liz's tone was bright and eager.

"I'll play Hearts," said Don. He pulled his chair up to the table. "I'll have some tea too, if I may."

"You may, indeed," said Liz. "I'll just get some cups."

The game was winding down an hour later when Allan came into the back porch stamping the snow from his overshoes. Gertrude had put Roderick to bed, much to that young man's dismay. "I want to stay up and see Annie and Grand," he'd protested.

"Not tonight," Gertrude had said. Her tone forbade argument.

"I always miss all the fun," had muttered Roderick to himself from under the bed covers.

"The snow's stopped and it's as clear as a bell out there." Allan hung his jacket behind the stove. "The moon's out and you can see for miles." He held his hands over the stove to warm them. "It's beautiful."

"Tea for you, Allan? It'll warm your insides."

"Thanks Liz." He rubbed his hands together to restore circulation. "I plowed as far as the brook. I had to use the tractor and blade, the snow was too deep for the snowblower to handle. It's pretty clear the rest of the way up to the road and I made a hole through the bank so we can get out tomorrow if the snow plow doesn't come and fill it in again tonight." He took the cup of tea from Liz and sipped carefully. "Where's Roderick?"

"Gone to bed under protest," chuckled Gertrude. "I figured he needed his sleep, because I know he'll be wanting to get outdoors and play in the snow tomorrow."

"How about a tune on the fiddle, Uncle Will?" asked Cassie.

"Sure, what'll it be tonight?" Will opened the violin case and took out the fiddle.

"'Soldier's Joy' and 'Brown Haired Maiden.'" said Cassie. "Then 'Minstrel Boy' and 'Annie Laurie.'"

"You want it all, do you?" Uncle Will laughed and tried the strings for tune. Satisfied with the tuning he slid easily into the opening bars of 'The Cradle Song.' "I have to warm up the fingers, you know. They're not as limber as they used to be."

Presently the notes of 'Soldier's Joy' filled the shadowed kitchen. Cassie's toes tapped in time. The music ran on and on and seemed to weave a spell over the listeners. The dark corners of the kitchen seemed to be peopled with grey figures. It's my imagination, thought Cassie. She tried to ignore what her eyes wanted to tell her.

"It's a shame we don't have room for an eightsome reel," said Liz, whose feet wouldn't stay still either.

'The Brown Haired Maiden' followed. Gertrude began to feel the gathering of forces outside themselves and watched anxiously with all her senses to see what would happen. I hope Eddy and Freddy are on the ball tonight, she thought. I don't want anything to happen to Roderick. She thought about her child upstairs, alone in the darkness with this gathering psychic storm in the kitchen. "We're here, Mother," echoed in her mind. She breathed a sigh of relief.

"Did you hear from Eddy and Freddy?" asked Don in a whisper.

Gertrude nodded. "Can you feel it too?"

"Yes," said the usually insensitive Don. "It must be strong if I can feel it."

"There's a lot of anger there," said Gertrude softly.

The slow sad music of 'The Minstrel Boy' filled the kitchen. Sad, more because of the words than the tune itself. 'Allan-a-Dare' soon followed. Cassie felt the hair on the back of her neck rise. She shivered. I don't know what's going on here tonight, she thought. It's really spooky! She glanced up at the warming oven on the stove. A faint glow surrounded it. She shook her head. It's just the chrome shining in the lamp light, she reassured herself. She looked at Liz to see if she was feeling uneasy too.

Liz was gazing at Uncle Will. My good-ness, he looks like Grand this evening, she thought. His features seemed to waver and become Grand's for a moment. Liz squeezed her eyes shut tight to clear her vision. She opened them again and looked over at Uncle Will. He looked like himself again. I guess it's not surprising, she thought, after all, they were brothers. She turned her attention to the music again.

The haunting melody of 'Annie Laurie' filled the air. The glow from the warming oven increased and took shape as Will pulled the melody from the old violin. The last notes hung tremulously in the silence until applause burst forth from the warming oven.

"It's a fine old tune," said Grand from his seat next to Annie. "It was always my favourite."

Everyone's head snapped around to face the stove. Aunt Maggie gurgled and fainted, her head hanging sideways onto her shoulder. Uncle Will sat frozen in his place staring at his brother.

"Hello, Dad," said Allan. "Long time, no see."

"Mind your manners, Allan," said Grand from his seat on the warming oven door. "I taught you better than that."

Allan subsided sullenly and muttered something unpleasant under his breath. Don and Gertrude sat back and observed.

"How nice to see you again, Grand," croaked Liz. "Would you like a cup of tea?"

"No, thanks, Liz, I can't drink tea here, but you're a good girl for asking. Cassie, help your old uncle down off this door, it's getting pretty hot up here."

Cassie gulped and tried not to shrink from his request. She got up from her chair and held out her hand to him. Grand laughed his familiar elfin chuckle. "That's okay, girl, you can't really help me from that side. I just wanted to see if you would." Cassie's sigh of relief was clearly audible to everyone there. She sat down again with a thump as Grand floated gently down from the oven door.

"So Will, have you been chasing any women

lately?" Grand sat down beside Allan on the lounge. Allan looked uneasily at his father and edged higher on the lounge. "Sit still, Allan!" said Grand, "I want to talk to your uncle. We have a lot to discuss."

Will set the fiddle down in its case. "I've been playing your fiddle these last few days, Grand. I hope you don't mind."

"I know," said Grand, "but that's not what I asked you." He stared at Will with ghostly eyes. Will seemed to shrink into his chair a little.

"What was it you wanted to know?" Will's voice quavered.

"I said, have you been chasing women lately?"

Will laughed. "I'm too old to be chasing women, Grand. I never was one much for chasing them anyway."

"Humph!" Grand turned his attention to Allan. "What're you doing here? I thought you'd said you'd never darken my door again."

"It isn't your door anymore," reminded Allan with a sudden flare of bravado.

"That's true enough," said Grand. "I keep forgetting." He glanced around the room. "I've brought Annie to see you. Come down here, Annie, and greet Allan."

Annie wafted gently down off the warming oven door. Will shrank from her as she passed him with barely a glance. She stood in front of Allan looking down at him with great sorrow in her eyes. She held out her hand to him but his hand passed right through hers and fell emptily into his lap.

"Not much good to you now, is she?" gibed Will, forgetting who he was dealing with.

Allan exploded. "You filthy old lecher, shut your mouth! It's all your fault she's dead." Allan's face contorted with rage.

"She was no good for you," said Will. "What did you want with a simpleton who couldn't talk?"

"She wasn't a simpleton," retorted Allan. "She was lovely, and she was learning to talk. She didn't want to tell anyone until she could do it well."

"So what?" asked Will. "She'd still be no good for anyone. She was only good for chasing butterflies and picking daisies."

"Well, you certainly saw to that! You'd be dead too if I could have gotten away with it, but you weren't worth it." Allan turned his attention back to Annie and gazed longingly at her.

"So Will, what do you have to say for yourself?" asked Grand. "Do you know why she died?"

"She slipped and fell into the brook down by the bridge where it's deepest."

"She didn't slip," said Grand. "She drowned herself from shame."

"From shame?" Allan stared hard at his father. "What shame did she have?"

"Will knows." Grand absorbed some of Allan's rage and turned toward Will. His wrath took on physical proportions and he seemed to increase in size as he loomed over Will in anger. "You will pay for this over and over again, Will, and no one can help you." His ethereal form engulfed Will's body. "What you have done is a terrible thing."

Will fought his way out of the enveloping mist of Grand's otherworldly form and ran screaming to the door. Wrenching the door open he raced coatless into the starry night and climbed into Allan's truck. He stalled it twice before the engine turned over and continued to run. He sped across the dooryard and down the freshly plowed lane. The surface was icy. Snow sprayed out from under the spinning tires.

"I hope he makes it to the road," said Liz who was the first one to find her voice.

"It's a four wheel drive," said Allan dully.

"What's happening? Why's the door wide open in the dead of winter? Where's Will?" spluttered Aunt Maggie as she returned to consciousness.

"Gone to town," said Grand, whereupon Aunt Maggie fainted again.

§

A subdued group gathered around the breakfast table the next morning. The sun sparkled on the frosted window panes, and made the kitchen bright with light reflected from the snow outside. A large bouquet of fresh daisies stood in warm water in a jam jar in the middle of the table. Aunt Maggie chose to ignore them. "Where's Will this morning?" she cackled. She seemed a smaller, older version of herself.

"Gone to town," replied Allan, echoing Grand's words of the night before.

Aunt Maggie looked at him sharply. "Now why'd he go to town so suddenly? I thought the roads were closed. His car'd never make it through."

Allan glared at her. "He didn't take his car," he almost snarled.

"Mind your tone with me, young man. Whose car'd he take?"

"He took my truck."

"Your truck? He doesn't know how to drive a truck."

"Well, he took it anyway." Allan pushed away from the table. "I'm going out to see if the lane's still clear."

The others continued their silent breakfast. Presently a knock came at the door. It was Cassie's Bob.

"G'day, Bob," said Liz. "We didn't hear you drive in. Come in out of the cold. Let me take your coat."

Bob handed her his coat. "I walked in from the road. I didn't know if the lane was plowed all the way to the house and I didn't want to take a chance and have to turn around or back out."

"Have you had your breakfast?" asked Cassie.

"Thanks, I have. Whose truck is in the brook down there?"

"What colour is it?" asked Liz carefully. She fought a sick feeling forming in the bottom of her stomach.

"Dark blue with silver stripes over the cab. It's in the water and there's not much sticking out. I hope no one was in it."

"I hope not either," said Liz. She reached for her coat. The others scrambled after her.

The little parade met Allan returning at a run from the brook. "My truck's in the bottom of the brook," he gasped, "and I think Uncle Will is in it!" He joined the group as they hurried to the bridge.

"You'll have to get a tractor to pull it out of there," said Bob surveying the situation from several angles. "Have you got one?"

"The Mounties'll have to be notified first before we do anything," said Cassie.

"It's a terrible thing to have happened, and just at Christmas too." Bob took Cassie's gloved hand. "Who is it they think is in the truck?"

"Uncle Will, Grand's brother," replied Cassie. She left her gloved hand in Bob's. She was quiet for a few minutes. "I thought you were just playing another of your practical jokes on us when you said there was a truck in the brook."

"I would never joke about such a thing! That's no joking matter!"

§

The Mounties came immediately and investigated efficiently. They supervised the work of pulling the truck from the brook. Will sat upright in the cab, a look of horror literally frozen on his face, his rigid fingers gripping the wheel, and his open eyes staring sightlessly into the unknown.

Cassie took one glance and with a little whisper buried her face in Bob's welcoming lapel. He put his arms around her and held her close.

The ambulance drivers walked in from the road carrying their stretcher. It was some time before they could pry Will's fingers from the steering wheel.

"Should've brought another blanket," muttered one. Will's frozen limbs stuck grotesquely in the air.

"Turn him on his side," said the other.

"Won't fit," grunted the other in his effort to comply.

They covered him as well as they could and trudged back up the lane with their burden.

"I guess this one's for autopsy, eh?" said the driver as they neared Charlottetown.

"I guess so. The cops said to take him to the mortuary." He glanced behind himself into the back of the ambulance. "Geez! Would you look at that!"

Will's arms had thawed sufficiently to slowly collapse into his frozen lap, the blanket in a tangle over his face and chest.

Chapter Ten

After the ambulance had left and the Mounties had satisfied themselves that this was an accident, the somber group made their way back to the house. For once Aunt Maggie had made herself useful and had stoked up the fire and made a pot of tea. Allan got the tow truck to haul his truck to a heated garage in Wood Islands to see if they could thaw it out. He came back to the house a few minutes later.

Aunt Maggie sat in the rocking chair sniffing and dabbing at her eyes. "So Will is gone too."

"Yes, Aunt Maggie, I know you'll miss him. You've known him for such a long time," said Liz.

"Ever since we were children. He was only two years older than me." She continued sniffing and dabbing. "Whatever made him take Allan's truck last night?"

Liz and Cassie exchanged glances. "He and Allan had a disagreement last evening. I expect it was his way of getting the better of Allan. He knew how Allan valued his truck." She closed her lips tightly and turned toward the pantry. "I'll just get dinner started."

"I'll set the table." Cassie followed her into the pantry and shut the door. "It's a good thing that she fainted last night."

"I wonder if Gertrude can shed any more light on what Will really did," said Liz. She tied on an apron and began peeling potatoes.

"Maybe this evening. Aunt Maggie will probably want to go to bed early." Cassie began counting silverware and napkins for the table.

§

The afternoon dragged by. No one had much to say except Aunt Maggie who kept inter-jecting remarks and reminiscences about Will into the heavy silence. Roddy played on the floor with his trucks and Mr. Dog. From the parlour the faint sound of wind chimes echoed from time to time. Everyone except Roddy ignored them. He finally tugged at Gertrude's sweater sleeve. "Mommy, Mommy, Annie is calling us," he whispered in a loud little boy whisper.

"Ssh," whispered Gertrude. "Tell her I'll talk to her this evening." She returned to the book she was reading. It was a Victorian novel about love gone wrong and barely held her attention. Presently she closed the book and stood up. "I'm going for a walk. Come with me, Don."

In a few minutes, she and Don had waded through the snow drifts to the shore and found a washed up log to sit on. The sky was a clear, cold blue and the waves still broke on the sand with the little energy left over from

the storm. Overhead, seagulls floated noisily,
ever hopeful of a hand out. The purple outline
of Nova Scotia fourteen miles away seemed to
float on the waters of the Strait. It was a glori-
ous day and seemed to be a present from the
universe for enduring the days of storm just
past. They sat silently hand in hand for awhile.

Presently Don asked, "D'you suppose
Annie will be able to tell you anything more
this evening if you contact her?"

"Maybe. Now that Will is gone perhaps she
has her voice back. Anyway, I've been thinking that if she could show it to me movie style
it might be easier for her. I don't know what
skills she has acquired since she was here."

"Maybe Molly could help her."

"If I can track her down. She's been particularly elusive this time. I haven't been able to
pin her down except for brief moments like
last night. She always seems to have something else on her agenda."

"I hope you can. I'm getting tired of hearing
bells all the time. They've been loud enough

that even I, in my mortal ignorance, can hear them."

Gertrude laughed and picked up a handful of fluffy snow and threw it at Don. "See, I told you. You have more sensitivity than you give yourself credit for."

Don threw a handful back. "But I'm not coming ghost busting with you."

Supper was finally over and Roddy was tucked into bed. Exhausted from a vigorous snowball fight with Bob in the afternoon, he fell right asleep. Even Aunt Maggie unknowingly obliged and went to bed early. Bob had left for town right after supper. Cassie had walked him to the road where he had left his car and watched him out of sight. The moon rode near the tops of the pine trees with Venus nearby. Cassie sighed and turned back toward the house.

As she neared the house it seemed to glow with a light from within. I guess we've got electricity again, she thought. She entered the porch and flipped the light switch. Nothing happened. She felt her way to the kitchen door by the light of the moon pouring through the window. Inside the kitchen the lamps were lit and Aunt Maggie was just closing the door behind herself on her way to bed.

"I thought we had electricity again," she said. She hung her coat behind the stove.

"Not a flicker," said Don. "I just hope the lamp oil holds out until we can get more."

"I bought lots," said Liz. "Don't forget I grew up around here and I know how long the power can be out after a storm like we had."

Gertrude came into the kitchen after seeing Roddy to bed. "He's out. Eddy and Freddy are keeping watch. I took their playing cards so you don't have to worry, Don. I think I'll try to contact Annie from the parlour. That's where she seems to be the most active."

"Why not here in the kitchen?" asked Liz. "It seems to be where Roddy sees her all the time."

"If I do, you guys will have to be very, very quiet. It's delicate work for me and the energy can't be interrupted. I wish Mary Ann were here. Don will have to spot for me this evening." She settled herself in the rocking chair across from the stove. "Not one whisper. Do you understand me?" The air seemed to take on a charge not unlike the charge in the fun house at the fair ground during Old Home Week. Everyone nodded and watched Gertrude. She leaned back and closed her eyes.

Outside the wind whined around the eaves and sent clouds scudding across the moon. Inside the fire snapped and crackled in the stove's firebox, casting flickers of light through the draft at the side. On the table the kerosene lamp seemed to dim just a little, then brighten as Gertrude drew several deep breaths and settled more deeply into the rocker. A glow formed on top of the warming oven. Gertrude opened her eyes and stared at the glow.

"Hello, Grand. It's nice to see you again. Are you here alone?"

The apparition nodded. "Annie's coming soon. She's had a hard time."

Gertrude nodded. "Will isn't there with you, is he?"

Grand looked sad. "No, but it's his own fault. I had no idea."

"We know that. It wasn't your fault," said Gertrude. "It wasn't Annie's fault here either. She was just being obedient. Can she talk yet?"

"No, not yet. We keep hoping. She keeps trying. I think she's preparing a sort of film for you so you'll understand."

"Maybe once she shows me the film it will release her to talk again." Gertrude shifted in her chair. The glow on the top of the warming oven brightened. Annie joined Grand. She pointed toward the ceiling. Gertrude looked up just as the film began. It projected onto the white ceiling in perfect clarity. Annie as a young girl picking daisies and skipping alongside Grand as he went to fetch the cows home for milking. She chattered away to him and he seemed to answer her. Gertrude listened with as much acuteness as she could muster. Annie seemed to be about six, a lively little sprite with red-gold curls, and tanned arms and legs.

"Your great Uncle Will is coming this evening," said Grand. "You probably don't remember him. You haven't seen him for awhile. You and Allan will have to be on your best behaviour while he's here."

"How long will he be here?"

"A couple of weeks while we do the haying."

"Oh, goody! Can I drive the horses?"

Grand laughed. "We'll have to ask them if they'll let you. I'm the only one who ever drives them."

"Oh, Grand, horses can't talk."

"Of course they can. You just have to know how to listen." Grand opened the pasture gate and began calling the cows. "Cup ..., cup ..., cup." The bushes down by the creek rustled and presently three cows walked single file toward the gate. Grand looked down at Annie. He wiggled his eyebrows at her. "See, I can talk to cows too."

Will arrived later that night. Annie didn't take to him like everyone thought she would. She seemed wary and retreated to the other side of the stove from him. She said little. The next day she followed him into the barn at his bidding. She never spoke again. The film went dark. The glow on top of the warming oven faded.

Gertrude stirred and blinked. "I wish Mary Ann were here. I need her energy."

"Can we talk now?" asked Liz.

"For now. I don't know if I have the strength to continue this evening. Is there any more tea? A cup with some sugar and milk in it might shore me up."

"So what were you seeing? Who were you talking to?" Cassie could hardly stay on the edge of her seat. "All we could hear were mutterings."

"I was talking with Grand first. He said Will wasn't there. Annie still can't talk but she came shortly with a movie that she began to show me. Gertrude related the contents of the film to the others. "... And then the scene faded. I guess I ran out of energy. I'll try again later. It's a lot easier when Mary Ann and I work together."

"You look exhausted," said Don. "Why don't we call Mary Ann in the morning and see if she has time to come over tomorrow evening."

"Maybe that's best. The store will be open then and we can call from there."

"Come in time for supper," said Gertrude to Mary Ann. "We eat well here and Liz is a great cook."

"D'you want me to bring Jim too?"

"If he wants to come. We don't really need him. We already know what's disturbing the atmosphere. Anyway, I thought he was away in Ontario with family for the holidays."

"He's due back today. I pick him up this afternoon. What time is supper?"

"About six. Aunt Maggie is here too. She's

a little strange. Maybe we can convince her to go to bed early." Gertrude chuckled. "Tell her she needs her beauty sleep."

"That bad, huh?"

"She's old and not pretty."

Mary Ann arrived late in the afternoon. She had Betsy, Jim's dog, with her but not Jim. Betsy was as big and shaggy as her master. She took up all of the front seat next to Mary Ann. She loved a ghost hunt.

Mary Ann peeled her chubby self out of the driver's seat and released Betsy from her seat belt.

"Jim didn't come?"

"No, he was tired and since you didn't really need him, he said he needed some rest. Betsy was eager though. I hope it's alright that I brought her."

"Yeah, she and Mr. Dog can have a romp. I'll let him out. He's getting entirely too lazy."

"So what are we doing?"

Gertrude called Mr. Dog out while she filled Mary Ann in on what they already knew.

"Sounds interesting. It must be pretty powerful if you needed me too."

They watched Mr. Dog and Betsy make acquaintance. After a few bows and tail waggings and a good nether sniff they were off and running.

"It is. Annie can't talk so she had to show me scenes like in a movie. She could talk until she was about six or seven, then all of a sudden she couldn't anymore. It seemed to correspond with a visit from Uncle Will that summer."

"And now she wants to get her story told." Mary Ann pursed her lips. "Where is Uncle Will now?"

"He died a couple of days ago. Drowned in the creek where Annie drowned a number of years ago. You crossed the bridge as you came in the lane."

"I thought it felt funny down there."

"C'mon in and meet the others. It's warmer

by the fire than standing out here. The dogs are okay to run. They'll come when they get hungry."

That evening after Aunt Maggie and Roddy were safely tucked into bed, Gertrude and Mary Ann settled themselves into the rockers.

"Now don't you go to sleep on me like you did before," said Gertrude.

"I won't. This is much too interesting. Besides it was only once."

Gertrude turned to the others. "You know the drill. Not a sound."

Together Gertrude and Mary Ann turned inward and the glow on top of the warming oven appeared and increased. Even those sitting silently around the edges of the kitchen could see it tonight.

Grand and Annie appeared within the glow. Annie was smiling. "Say hello to Allan for me," she said.

Gertrude almost opened her eyes at the

sound of Annie's voice.

Annie nodded. "I can talk a little. I've been silent for so long I don't have much strength yet, so you'll have to listen closely. Grand can help me. I am going to show you the rest of the movie." She pointed to the ceiling once more. Gertrude and Mary Ann looked up. It was a scene from long ago. It took place around the farm and only they could see it. Everyone else sat silently staring at the blank ceiling.

Gertrude and Mary Ann watched and listened as Annie wandered along the shore. The pink sand was warm on her bare toes, and the summer sun was hot on her thin back. The wreath of daisies she'd woven earlier to wear in her red-gold hair had wilted and was now drooping over one ear giving her an almost elfin look. Overhead the seagulls called raucously to each other as they wheeled and dipped on the updrafts over the ocean.

Annie stooped to examine a clam shell,

its inside a translucent pink, its edges worn from the waves and the sand. She dropped it into her pocket to save for a souvenir of the summer. A smile lit her delicate features as she stood for some moments lost in thought. She startled when the ferry from the mainland tooted its arrival down the shore at Wood Islands. She squinted against the bright sun trying to identify which boat was arriving, but the distance was too great to see its distinguishing features. She watched until it disappeared behind the breakwater, then stood staring across the Northumberland Strait at the purple hills that marked the mainland of Nova Scotia.

Her walk continued until a certain maturing of the afternoon light told her it was time for chores. She turned and ran back across the sandy shore to the cow pasture. She clapped her hands and the cows lifted their heads from the lush grass and ambled over to her, still chewing the last green mouthful. She led them home across the field, and they went single file into the barn, where they found their stalls and stood patiently while she fastened the stanchions around their necks.

She began scooping feed into the mangers. Presently Allan came into the barn. "Hello, Annie," he said softly. She smiled radiantly at him.

Grand, coming through the door behind Allan, caught their greeting.

"Annie! Go help your aunt in the kitchen." Grand's tone was sharp.

Annie looked surprised and a little hurt. She set down the bucket of feed and left the barn. At the house the screen door slammed behind her and bounced on its hinges.

"Oh, it's you, is it, Annie?" said Aunt Lizzie. "Are they finished milking this soon?"

Annie shook her head.

"Well, since you're here, you can set the table while I finish whipping this cream. It doesn't seem to want to whip this evening. I've been at it so long I'm afraid I'll soon have butter." Aunt Lizzie turned back to her task.

Annie set the table then wandered back outdoors into the late afternoon sunshine. Presently she returned with a bouquet of Queen Anne's Lace and wild roses. Clutching the bouquet she rummaged in a cupboard in the back porch for a jam jar to use for a vase. She carried the jar into the kitchen and filled it with warm water from the water tank on the end of the stove and then stuffed the flowers into it.

"Well, now, Annie, that's right pretty," said Aunt Lizzie as Annie set the flowers in the centre of the table. "You're a good girl to think of that."

Annie smiled and patted her Aunt's plump hand.

"Oh, dear, here's Grand and Allan and I still have to mash the potatoes." Aunt Lizzie scurried into the pantry with the pot of potatoes and carefully drained them into the slop bucket. She mashed them and added a large helping of butter and a little milk. "There now, that should do it," she muttered to herself.

She turned them into the serving bowl and brought them to the table.

"Sit in then, Annie, they'll be along in a minute." Aunt Lizzie sat down at the end of the table nearest to the pantry. Grand and Allan took their usual places. Everyone bowed their heads. "For what we are about to receive may the Lord make us truly grateful and pardon our sins, in Jesus' name, amen," intoned Grand.

Knives and forks clattered as plates were readied. "Pass the meat to Grand and Allan, Annie. I'll start the vegetables. Did you get the big field finished this afternoon, Allan?"

"Most of it," replied Allan around a mouthful of mashed potatoes. "We'll have to ted it tomorrow, it's still a little damp." He looked across the table at Annie and smiled. Grand and Aunt Lizzie exchanged glances. Aunt Lizzie folded her lips tightly and Grand nodded slightly. Supper continued in silence.

Presently Aunt Lizzie said, "Annie picked strawberries this afternoon. She knows where to find the early ones. I made some whipped cream to go with them." She began passing the bowls of wild strawberries. "Pour the tea, would you, please, Annie?"

"Will and Murdoch are coming out tomorrow to help us with the hay," said Grand. "The early spring gave us a head start on the harvest."

"I suppose Maggie'll come too," replied Aunt Lizzie. She didn't know whether to sigh or smile so she did neither, and only succeeded in looking disapproving. "Maggie's a great talker," she said. "And always on about nothing. Oh, well." The sigh escaped after all. "She'll be company, I suppose, and a change."

"I expect so. Murdoch can't get out the door without her coming too," said Grand. "She'll be company for the day anyway."

Some of the joy went out of Annie's face. She shivered slightly.

"What's the matter Annie? Did you get a chill down on the shore today?" asked Aunt

Lizzie. She put her hand on Annie's fore-head."You're not running a fever, so what's all the shivering about?"

Annie looked back at Aunt Lizzie and shook her head.

"I hope you're not sickening for anything," she said gruffly. She stroked Annie's golden red curls. "We'd have a hard time getting you back to town without a car."

Annie smiled and patted Aunt Lizzie's hand.

"I think Allan's sweet on Annie," said Grand that night as he and Aunt Lizzie were getting ready for bed.

"You'd better have a talk with him, then." Aunt Lizzie braided her hair into a thick plait for the night. "Annie's a fine girl, but she's simple and she'll never be anything else."

"It's a terrible shame." Grand pulled his nightshirt over his head. "She's such a beauty. Liz and Cassie'll never have her looks." The bed springs squeaked as he sat down heavily on his side of the bed. "Strange thing that. One day she was fine, babbling away and full of questions like any six year old and the next, not a word out of her."

"Nor any since, either." Aunt flung her braid behind her back. "The doctors couldn't make head nor tail of it." She began pulling loose hair out of her hairbrush.

"Ah, well, what's done is done, whatever happened." Grand sighed. "Come to bed now, Lizzie, so I can blow out the lamp."

Murdoch, Maggie and Will arrived early the next morning. The day had dawned with a brilliant blue sky overhead. Fat summer clouds moved across it pushed by the salt breeze from the Strait. The crows cawed from the spruce bush behind the house. The house was old and had settled enough on its red sandstone foundations to look as if it had grown there like the mushrooms that grew in the damp places in the yard.

"Come in, come in, and welcome!" exclaimed Aunt Lizzie. "Allan and Grand are just finishing chores. Have you had breakfast?"

"Yes, before we left home." Maggie settled herself in Aunt Lizzie's place at the table. "A cup of tea will not come amiss."

Aunt Lizzie suppressed a sigh. "You must have made a real early start to be here already." She pushed the kettle onto the firebox of the stove.

"About six-fifteen. Murdoch and Will were that eager to get going."

"Annie, go get a pitcher of milk for the porridge, like a good girl, please."

"My, she's certainly growing up fast," observed Maggie, when she judged Annie to be out of earshot. "It's a real shame she's simple like that." She brushed at a stray crumb on the table.

"Yes, and who's to look after her when we pass on, I'd like to know." Aunt Lizzie wiped the table with more energy than was necessary. She began spreading cutlery around.

"She can look after herself well enough but she doesn't know a thing. Her mother's been sick ever since the last one and can't take care of her, and Liz and Cassie are too young."

Maggie nodded. "And not being able to talk like that ..." Her voice trailed away as Annie returned with the pitcher of milk.

"So, Annie, are they nearly finished milking?" asked Aunt Lizzie.

Annie nodded.

"I'll start the bacon." Aunt Lizzie pulled the cast iron frying pan out of the warming oven. It was blackened from years of use and was well seasoned from the many rashers of bacon cooked in it over the years. "I was going to set bread today, but since you're here, I guess I'll wait. I have enough until tomorrow."

"Don't wait on my account," said Maggie. "I haven't had anything but boughten bread since the children went out on their own. I like a nice slice of homemade bread."

§

In the end the relatives stayed for three days. Annie spent her free time picking the last of the early strawberries and roaming about the shore. On the last evening Allan found her there. She was sitting on the edge of a little sandstone cliff just under the bank staring moodily across the Strait watching the ferry from the mainland coming into port at Wood Islands. Allan climbed up from the shore and sat down beside her.

"Hello, Annie." His voice was gentle. "I'm sorry I couldn't come to you these last few days." He sighed. "Grand has kept me very busy with chores."

Annie turned and looked at him. A tiny smile crossed her lips and she leaned against Allan's solid young shoulder and patted his hand.

"Grand told me not to spend time with you anymore. That people might misinterpret it."

Annie looked up at him with a question in her eyes.

"He said that people might think that I was,

well, um, using you." Allan's blush showed through his tan. "You know."

Annie's lips formed an 'oh'. She smiled up at him and relaxed against him.

Allan looked down at her happy open face and shook his head. "Oh, Annie, I don't think you understand at all. Maybe Grand was right. I should stay away from you."

Annie's eyes widened in alarm. She shook her head. "No!" she said quite plainly, then looked startled by her outburst.

Allan gasped. He turned her face around to look into her eyes. "Did you say no?" he asked in disbelief.

Annie nodded.

"Can you say it again?"

Annie struggled with the word, and finally shook her head, an expression of sadness crossing her face.

"If you could say it once, you can say it again," said Allan. "And if you can say no, you can say other things too. I'm going to tell Grand about this."

Annie tugged at his sleeve shaking her head in alarm.

"No?" Allan frowned in disbelief. "But you want to be able to talk, don't you?"

Annie nodded forlornly.

"Don't you think you think you can?"

Annie shrugged.

"Annie, if you can say one word, you can say others," persisted Allan. "You need to get help to learn how."

She shook her head again.

A look of frustration crossed Allan's face. "Well, I can't help you then!" He folded his arms across his chest.

Annie nodded vigorously and tugged on his sleeve, her face alight with enthusiasm.

"No!" Allan stared down into her excited face. "You think I can?" He frowned.

Annie nodded happily.

"Can I tell Grand and Aunt Lizzie what we're doing?"

Annie shook her head adamantly.

"You want to keep it a secret?"

She nodded again.

"Well," said Allan slowly, "I'll try. But at the end of the summer, if you haven't learned to say any words, I'm going to tell Grand."

Annie's blue eyes darkened and she nodded slowly. They sat quietly watching the ferry making its way back to Caribou.

Gertrude watched the turmoil of Allan's thoughts as they crossed his face. She listened hard with her psychic ears.

I hope this works, he thought, though I don't know how I can keep it from Grand all summer. He thought back to his and Grand's conversation of two days ago. He remembered his embarrassment. Why did Grand have to bring up Annie, and in front of Uncle Will too! He remembered how Grand had sent Annie into the house to help Aunt Lizzie get supper ready.

"Allan, I don't think you should spend so much time with Annie." Grand got right to the point once Annie was gone.

"Why not?" asked Allan. "We've always spent a lot of time together in the summer time."

"You're not children anymore." Grand lifted a forkful of last year's straw into a stall and spread it around. "I think you should keep your distance."

Uncle Will snickered. "She's growing up into a fine looking woman and people will talk."

Allan's cheeks grew red with embarrassment, and then rage as he realized the implication of his uncle's words. "I would never hurt Annie!"

"Now, son, I know you wouldn't," said Grand, "but people have nasty minds." He stared pointedly at Will.

"Yes," said Will, "people will be thinking you can have a roll in the hay any time you want it." He snickered again. "If they're thinking it, they'll soon be saying it." Allan had felt his insides curl at his uncle's words.

§

Allan put his arm around Annie and drew her close. The perfume of her hair floated gently into his awareness. She's so fragile, he thought. It's a wonder someone like this could even live. His thoughts turned again to Will's insinuations. I wonder what it would be like to make love with her. He felt an internal stirring and blushed at where his thoughts had led him. He shifted restlessly where he sat. Annie looked up at him questioningly, her blue gaze intent and trusting on his face. He blushed more hotly still, and avoided her eyes. She will be beautiful, he thought. Gertrude smiled.

Annie spent a great deal of time alone that fall. The speech lessons with Allan had ceased. He was angrily silent, answering only in mono-syllables when spoken to. The only time she saw him was at dinner and supper, when he would not meet her eyes across the table. She began going for solitary walks after she over-heard Aunt Lizzie say to Grand one day that

Allan was seeing a girl from the Harbour. He came home smelling of liquor more nights than not, and was surly and unpleasant the next morning.

Annie grew pale and listless in the following weeks. She seemed to be in mourning, but Aunt Lizzie was unable to discover the reason. A bout of vomiting caught her unawares one morning as she swept the kitchen floor. She dropped the broom and ran outdoors with her hand covering her mouth trying to contain the bilious return from her stomach. After the spasm was over she collapsed in the rocking chair on the outside porch shivering in the cold October air.

Aunt Lizzie brought her a jacket. "Here, put this on before you catch your death of cold."

Annie patted her Aunt's hand to thank her and obediently put the jacket on.

"Has this happened before?" asked Aunt Lizzie.

Annie shook her head and leaned back in the chair, closing her eyes.

"Has your time of the month come lately?"

A frightened look crossed Annie's pale features. She shook her head.

Aunt Lizzie sighed. "Ah, well, there's nothing that can be done about it now." She sighed again. "I don't know what I'll say to your parents."

Annie sat up in alarm and shook her head vehemently.

"But they'll have to know sooner or later," said Aunt Lizzie, "and you certainly can't tell them."

Annie shook her head again and began to cry silently.

"D'you want to go home?"

She shook her head slowly and scrubbed at her eyes with a scrap of tissue she found in her jacket pocket.

"Well, I guess it's really our problem since it happened here, and the fewer people to know the better, and your mother isn't well enough to deal with this." Aunt Lizzie sat lost in thought for some minutes. "That

Allan should be horse-whipped for fooling around with you!" She went into the house and slammed the door.

Annie sat on the porch for some time until at last the cold drove her indoors again. She hung her jacket on the hook behind the stove and went over to Aunt Lizzie. She put her slim young arms around her and patted her gently on her back.

Aunt Lizzie returned her embrace. "Oh, Annie, if I could only make this easier for you."

October continued cool and rainy. The few remaining leaves drifted to the ground and were piled by the wind into sodden heaps around the fences and the buildings. Annie's condition was concealed for a time by her loose-fitting aprons and dresses. Aunt kept silent until Grand observed one day that Annie was putting on a little weight.

"It's not weight she's putting on, replied Aunt Lizzie gruffly. "She's in the family way."

"Tsk, tsk," clucked Grand, "what'll we do now?"

"I suppose sometime, sooner or later I'll have to tell her parents, though I don't know what in the universe I'll say." Aunt Lizzie shook her head and sighed.

"Yes, and it'll probably be sooner rather than later," said Grand. "I wish Allan had left her alone!"

Aunt Lizzie sighed again. "No use crying over spilt milk now. I'll write to Elizabeth after Thanksgiving and she and Dan can decide what they want to do for their daughter. Murdoch and Maggie'll be here tomorrow for the weekend and I suppose Will'll likely be with them."

"Yes, and he'll have plenty to say about it too, or I'll miss my guess."

"Och, that fellow should have been married all his life and had a pack of children, then he'd know what it's like to try to keep ahead of them," said Aunt Lizzie. Her upper lip curled in distaste for Will and his attitude.

§

Thanksgiving weekend brought snow flurries and a cold wind. Murdoch and Maggie arrived late Saturday afternoon accompanied by the ubiquitous Will.

"That wind'll cut you like a knife," said Murdoch. "We'll be having snow before too long."

"Not too soon, I hope." said Grand. "The winter's long enough without it starting to snow in October." He turned and led the way into the house.

"Welcome, welcome!" exclaimed Aunt Lizzie. "Hang your coats behind the stove and sit down. I'll just make a pot of tea to warm you. It'll be ready in a minute or two. I set a fire in the parlour stove, Grand. Take the men in there while I have a visit with Maggie." She hustled the men toward the parlour. "Have you been to town lately, Maggie?"

"Charlottetown?" asked Maggie taking out the inevitable knitting.

"Yes, I was just wondering if you'd seen Elizabeth and Dan lately."

"No, but we had word there a few weeks ago that she still hasn't recovered her strength."

"That was a serious operation she had after the baby was stillborn, so I'm not surprised. Has she got any help around the house?"

"She doesn't need it. That little Liz is as good a housekeeper as she'd ever want, and her only eleven. I guess she can bake and cook almost as well as Elizabeth can. She keeps that place spotless and goes to school too."

"Who looks after Cassie?"

"Liz. Cassie's in school now too, and she comes and goes with Liz every day. Liz is a wonderful help. A real credit to her mother."

"Well, who'd have thought that Liz'd turn out to be such a help, and her so young. Elizabeth hardly ever expected anything of her, and she always seemed so childish. Of course, I haven't seen her since last fall, so maybe her mother's illness was the making of her."

"Elizabeth's been ailing since before last

Christmas, so I expect Liz has learned a lot this year." Maggie rummaged in her knitting bag for a new ball of yarn. "Where's Annie?"

"Around somewhere," replied Aunt Lizzie. She spooned tea leaves into the teapot and poured boiling water over them. She shoved the teapot to the side of the stove to steep. A little of the water splashing out of the spout fell, hissing, onto the hot stove. "She's expecting."

"Expecting? How? Who?"

"It's Allan's and I expect they did it the usual way," said Aunt Lizzie.

"Does her mother know?" For once Maggie's hands were still, lying idly in her aproned lap.

"No, and you're not to tell her either."

Maggie's face fell slightly. "Oh, well, I wouldn't think of being the bearer of news like that."

Wouldn't you just, thought Aunt Lizzie.

Gertrude smiled at Aunt Lizzie. You certainly have Aunt Maggie's number, she thought.

Aunt Lizzie trudged off to the pantry to get cups and saucers. "I made an applesauce cake this morning. We'll have a little of it with our tea. I just have to ice it."

"When are you going to tell her mother?"

"Not until I have to. Her health's so precarious I don't want to upset her if I can help it, although I don't see how it can be avoided."

Annie did not put in an appearance until nearly supper time. Aunt Lizzie went in search of her and found her huddled under the quilt in her bedroom. "Come down now and have a bite to eat, Annie."

Annie shook her head.

"Now, child, you'll have to face them sometime. So why not do it now and get it over with?"

Annie looked up bleakly from her nest of covers.

"Are you afraid of what they'll say?"

Annie shook her head.

"What, then?"

"Momma," Annie mouthed the word but no sound came out.

"Your mother?"

Annie nodded.

"I've sworn Maggie to secrecy on that point, so you don't need to worry. She likes coming here too much to break that promise," said Aunt Lizzie grimly. "Now brush your hair and come down and have some supper. You can't grow a baby without eating at least for one."

Annie did as she was told, appearing in the kitchen a few minutes later and sliding quickly into her chair.

"Here she is," said Will, "as beautiful as ever."

His voice boomed on Annie's ears and she cringed.

Aunt Lizzie raised an eyebrow at Grand across the table. He responded with an almost imperceptible shake of his grey head. Aunt sighed. "Return thanks, please, Grand."

Grand bowed his head. "For what we are about to receive may we be truly thankful, bless it to our use and pardon our sins. Amen."

"Amen," everyone chorused after a moment of silence.

"Start the meat, Grand. Everyone help themselves to whatever's in front of them and pass it along."

For some minutes the silence in the kitchen was broken only by the sound of forks and knives on plates and the crackle of the fire in the stove. Despite being a person of large appetite and unpleasant table manners, Will finished first. He pushed his plate aside and leaned on his elbows, taking note of the ever silent Annie.

"What's the matter with you, Annie. You're awful pale today."

"She hasn't been well these last few weeks," replied Aunt Lizzie. "Have some more, Will." She passed him the bowl of carrots. "Grand, pass the meat and potatoes to Will. The gravy is right in front of you, Will."

"Had the flu, did she?"

"Something like that," said Aunt Maggie. She dumped an overload of carrots onto Will's plate.

"I can't eat all that," he protested. "Give

some to Maggie."

Aunt Lizzie picked the top ones off and put them back in the dish. "More carrots, Maggie?"

"I don't mind if I do. A little more potato and some gravy wouldn't come amiss either." Maggie heaped her plate high a second time.

"It's great to have your appetite, Maggie," teased Will. "If we ever have a famine you'll be the last to go."

Maggie glared at him. "It takes a lot of fuel to run a body this size."

"Your body wouldn't be that size if you didn't give it so much fuel," said Will.

"At least I don't get sick," snapped Maggie. "Besides, Murdoch likes me this way, don't you, Murdoch?"

"Oh, aye, you're a fine figure of a woman, that's for sure." He scraped the last of his potatoes and gravy from his plate.

Maggie tucked into her second helping.

"Leave room for dessert," said Aunt Lizzie. "I made a lemon pie this morning. Annie, help me clear the table, please."

Annie turned frightened, pleading eyes toward her aunt.

"Come now, Annie, there's a good girl."

Annie rose and began gathering plates and cutlery. She picked up the pile and turned to go into the pantry, revealing her profile to Will and the others.

Will's face took on a sly look. "So you've had the flu, have you, Annie?"

Annie nodded and hurried into the pantry.

"The kind of flu that comes from pretty close contact, I'd say," said Will. "So you didn't heed our advice, eh, Allan?"

"Shut up!" Allan grabbed his jacket from behind the stove and stomped out of the house.

A stunned silence followed his departure. "I'm truly sorry for the way my son spoke to you, Will," said Grand. His tone was formal. "He knows better than that, and I'll have him apologize when he returns."

"Here, Annie, pass this pie around," said Aunt. "Allan'll get over his snit and be back pretty soon."

Annie served pie without looking at anyone, then scuttled back to the pantry looking paler and more miserable than ever. She returned a few minutes later with the teacups and saucers.

"So you're going to be a Mommy," said Will.

Annie nodded miserably.

"What kind of mother will you make, I wonder? You won't be able to talk to it, though that may be a blessing in disguise. At least you won't be able to nag at it like my mother always did with us."

"Now, Will, our mother was a good woman and she did the best she knew how," said Grand.

"I know, I know, I'm just having a little fun at Annie's expense."

"Well don't," said Aunt Lizzie. "She has enough to bear now without you adding to it."

Will lapsed into silence for a few minutes. Then, "Maybe the kid won't be able to talk either," he muttered.

Annie jumped up and left the table. She hurried upstairs where the others could hear her pacing in her room.

"Let's have a tune, Grand," said Will. "I brought my guitar this time."

The guitar and violin covered up the sounds of Annie's footsteps. Aunt Lizzie thought several times of going up to see her but refrained. Gertrude listened in. I wish that Will would keep his nasty mouth shut, thought Aunt Lizzie. Annie didn't need that and neither did Allan. I hope Allan comes in soon, it's going to be an awful cold night. Not a good one for spending in the barn, if that's where he is.

The music ceased about eleven o'clock. "I'm played out," said Grand. He loosened his bow. "That was a good tune."

Aunt Lizzie pushed the kettle over onto the front of the stove where it began to sing. "We'll just have a cup of tea and a biscuit before we go to bed." She bustled around preparing night lunch. I'd better go up and check on Annie, she thought. I'll bring her a little bite so she won't have to come down. She hardly ate any supper at all.

She made up a plate and warmed some milk then hurried upstairs with it, only to find an empty room. She lifted her lamp high to eliminate the worst of the shadows. "Annie? Where are you, Annie?" She searched the upstairs. Annie wasn't there. She hurried down to the kitchen. "Annie's not in her room!"

"Where is she then?" Grand frowned.

"Probably gone off to the barn to be with Allan," said Will. "I wouldn't put it past her."

Grand and Aunt Lizzie both glared at Will. "If you'd have left her alone, none of this would've happened," said Aunt Lizzie.

"She may be in the parlour," said Maggie. "The stove's on in there so it's warm. Did you look in there?"

"I'll go now." Aunt Lizzie set the plate on the table and picked up the lamp. She hurried across the hall to the parlour. It was empty. She searched the other rooms and finally returned to the kitchen without Annie. "She's nowhere to be found."

"Well, she can't have gone out in the cold,"

said Murdoch. "Her coat's still here."

"She must still be in the house. She wouldn't go out without her coat. I'll just look again." Aunt Lizzie picked up the lamp again. I wish we had electricity up here, she thought, but Grand's so stubborn.

She returned a few minutes later. "She's just not here, and her heavy sweater's gone from her drawer."

"At least she didn't go out without anything on." Maggie set down her knitting needles. "Will may be right. She may just be in the barn with Allan."

Grand shrugged into his heavy coat. "That's still not enough to be out running around in in this weather. She'll catch her death of pneumonia. Allan should have better sense, even if she doesn't." He stomped into his boots and strode out to the barn.

"Allan! Are you here, Allan?" Something stirred in the hay-scented darkness. "Is that you?" Grand peered into the gloom, a little startled when Allan's form, made bulky by his overcoat and several layers of horse blanket, loomed out of the empty stall.

"What do you want?"

"Is Annie with you?"

"No, and she hasn't been. Why?"

"She's not in the house, and she only took her heavy sweater with her."

"We'll have to look for her." Allan threw off his blanket and headed for the door. "Where does Aunt Lizzie keep the flashlights?" He hurried off in the direction of the house. "How long's she been gone?"

"We don't know. We were having a bit of a tune, and she must have slipped out then without us hearing her." Grand hurried to keep up with Allan's long strides.

"If she went out the front door, she'll have left tracks. I didn't get around to cleaning the snow off the front step today."

"Thank goodness!" Grand's breath came in hard pants in his effort to keep up. "There's only a little down but maybe it's enough so we can at least see where she went."

Grand, Allan, Murdoch and Will collected up flashlights and closely inspected the fine dusting of snow at the front door.

"She seems to be headed toward the lane," said Will.

Grand frowned. "I wonder if she took it into her head to try to walk to Charlottetown?"

Allan groaned. "She'd never make it." He watched the ground carefully, hampered by the weak beam in his light.

The others trudged down the lane after him. At the bridge Annie's footprints veered to the left and disappeared.

"Oh, no, Annie! No!" Allan scrambled over the bank and began tugging at the sodden form in the water, to no avail. Will and Grand joined him, and together they pulled Annie's lifeless body from the brook. Ice had already begun to form around the edges of her favourite rose-coloured sweater. Allan pushed the others aside and picked up her stiff little body, cradling it in his strong arms as he carried her back to the house, unaware of the tears that ran down his cheeks and froze on the edge of his scarf.

Allan sat pale and serious, between Aunt Lizzie and Grand at the little church where he had attended all his life. The dark circles under his eyes gave him an owlish look. Annie's parents and her sisters, Liz and Cassie, occupied the pew ahead of them. The other pews were filled with the relatives of their extended family and as many neighbours and friends as could find a seat. Annie had been well-loved for her sweetness and her gentle ways.

The hymns washed over the family, barely perceived in the grief. "Jesus loved the little children, for he said one day, let the children come unto me, keep them not away." Elizabeth broke down into a wild fit of weeping, abruptly cut off by her wadded handkerchief. Liz moved closer and put her childish arms around her mother's bowed shoulders.

It was Annie's favourite, thought Allan. He brushed away a few tears of his own.

The funeral service was brief, appropriate to Annie's short life. The mourners filed past the open casket for a last glimpse of their Annie. "She looks so natural," whispered one of the neighbours, "just like she would sit up and smile like she used to."

"She was a great one for smiling, all right," agreed another. "It's too bad she had to fall in the brook and it that cold. She must have perished instantly."

"It's a good thing she did, for it was an awful cold night that night. I wonder what she was doing out at that hour anyway?"

"Well, you know Annie, always roaming and rambling around the countryside even after dark."

"Her poor mother's taking it hard, and her not well, either. It's a good thing she's got Liz and Cassie. That Liz'll be a real comfort to her."

"It's her Aunt Liz who's taking it harder.

Annie was in her care all summer, and then to have this happen, and to have to tell her mother." The woman shook her head.

Annie's casket was carried into the little graveyard beside the church and carefully lowered into the grave beside her family who had gone before. "It's a good thing the ground hasn't frozen yet," muttered the grave digger to himself, "else she'd be above ground until spring." The biting wind from the Strait promised rain. The graveside service was mercifully brief. The congregation dispersed quickly to their homes.

Chores were a silent event that evening. Allan and Grand worked side by side without speaking. Maggie, Murdoch and Will had gone home after the funeral, and without Annie's happy presence, the worked seemed a joyless burden.

After an equally silent supper, Allan retired to the parlour and lit a fire in the stove. The room was cold from having been closed off without heat for the last few days while Annie's remains waited for their final disposal. The sawhorses that had supported Annie's casket still stood in awkward poses by the parlour windows. Allan carried them outside and set them on the front porch. He returned to the parlour and sat down in the armchair next to the stove. The weariness of the last few days lay heavily on him and he closed his eyes. Presently Grand joined him.

"It's hard to believe she won't be here anymore." Sadness filled Allan's voice.

"It is that," said Grand. He sat silently for awhile. "The one I feel worst for is her poor mother. She sent Annie to us in good faith for us to look after and look what happened. They said she was just distraught when she heard the news."

"I can imagine," said Allan. "I'm just glad she won't ever know Annie's condition. We were lucky to be able to cover her with flowers."

Grand looked across at Allan. "There

needn't have been anything to cover. Oh, Allan, why'd you have to go and do such a thing, especially to our Annie?"

Allan shifted in his seat. "I didn't."

"Will said he saw you with her in the barn."

"I wasn't with her in the barn."

"Allan, Allan, to do such a thing and then lie about it."

"So I'm a liar, am I?' Allan stared at his hands folded tightly in his lap.

"It does seem that way," said Grand sadly. "I thought I'd brought you up better than that, but I guess I haven't. Maybe breeding does matter the most."

"What's that supposed to mean?" asked Allan.

Grand pressed his lips together and didn't reply.

"What's that supposed to mean?"

Grand was silent for long minutes, then said, "I guess I should've told you before now." Grand paused then said in a rush, "You're not a MacLean."

Allan wrapped his arms around his midriff and leaned forward. "D'you mean Mom is not my real mother?" His voice was strained, barely above a whisper.

"No, and I'm not your real father." Grand stared at the fire flickering in the grate.

Allan rocked himself back and forth for long minutes, groaning as if in pain. "Why didn't you tell me?" he whispered at last.

"I thought you knew. Everyone else does."

Allan groaned again. "How could I know if no one told me?" He stopped rocking and slumped back in the chair. "Who is my real mother?" He held himself rigidly waiting for Grand's reply.

"Lizzie's sister, Mary, your aunt. You've never met her. She lives in New Brunswick now. We're not sure where anymore. For all we know she may have moved anywhere."

"And my father?"

"A French boy from Edmonston. He was here for the summer and met Mary. They were supposed to get married, but when he found out she was expecting, he abandoned her."

"Just like I did to Annie." Allan's pain was almost tangible. "If only I'd stood by her, she'd still be alive."

"It would seem so," said Grand, "but there's nothing can be done about that now. What's done is done, though I don't see why you had to go and fool around with Annie of all people. She was simple and your cousin to boot."

"She wasn't my cousin," Allan pointed out, "and she wasn't simple." He rose stiffly from his seat by the stove and climbed the stairs like an old man. Grand could hear him walking around overhead.

"This'll haunt you to the end of your days," he muttered. Sadness was heavy in his voice.

Allan left that night. He walked steadily toward Wood Islands until well after midnight, the cold wind a punishment in itself. He spent the rest of the night in a convenient barn and rose early enough to catch the first boat in the morning. A few days later Aunt Lizzie received a postcard from Fredricton. Allan had a job and a place to live. There was no return address. Each year at Christmas and on her birthday she received a card with only his signature. They continued for several years after her passing until Allan had received news of her death. Then the cards ceased.

Grand lived for ten years after Aunt Lizzie. He never spoke of Allan nor expressed any desire to see him again, although there was a certain sadness in his demeanour that hadn't been there before. It never left him.

Gertrude sighed and came out of trance. "So that's what happened," she said.

"Wow, what a sad story!" Mary Ann sat up straight in the rocker.

The glow on the top of the warming oven did not fade. Gertrude glanced up at it still dazed from her trance. "I think they have more to say." She closed her eyes and was instantly back with Grand and Annie.

"Tell Allan I'm very sorry that I blamed him. It grieves me to the core that I could have been so blind," said Grand. "I hope he can forgive me."

"Tell Allan that I love him now and I loved him back then," whispered Annie. "I wish I could have talked. None of this could have happened if I'd been able to tell what Will had done to me. I barely knew myself. I just knew it was wrong." Tears overflowed her eyelids. "He started when I was six and just kept it up every chance he got. I wasn't even safe in my own room at night."

"At least you won't have to worry about Will anymore," said Grand. "None of us will."

"None of us?" asked Gertrude.

"None of us. He's been relegated to a different, less comfortable area and he can't cross over to where we are. He can see us but he is cut off. If I'd known I'd have cut him from the family before he died. He would never have gotten to our Annie."

The glow on the warming oven began to fade. "It was good to see you all together again." Grand's voice began to diminish and his form became misty. Annie stood waving goodbye. "Thanks, Gertrude," she whispered.

"You're welcome, Annie" Gertrude blinked and sat up straight. A sniffling sound came from the corner of the lounge. Allan had his head buried in his arms and cried quietly for his Annie and what might have been if it hadn't been for Will.

Gertrude went to him. "Grand asked for your forgiveness." She handed Allan a handful of tissues. "Annie said to tell you that she loved you then and she loves you now."

Allan sat up and wiped his nose and eyes. "I'll have to think about all of it." He sniffed again. "How did Annie look? Was she well? Where was Will?"

"Annie looked radiant and she can talk again. Grand looked like himself only younger. Will was nowhere where I could see him. Grand said he was somewhere safe and couldn't get out to harm anyone again. Or at least for the time being."

"My poor Annie." Allan's tears overflowed again. A soft thump sounded from the centre of the table. A jar of daisies in warm water had appeared and sat glowing in the lamplight. The atmosphere felt suddenly lighter.

www.ingramcontent.com/pod-product-compliance
Lightning Source LLC
Chambersburg PA
CBHW052031020726
47501CB00004B/1353